Storylandia

The Wapshott Journal of Fiction

Issue 17

The Wapshott Press

Storylandia, Issue 17, The Wapshott Journal of Fiction, ISSN 1947-5349, ISBN 978-1-942007-04-3, is published at intervals by the Wapshott Press, PO Box 31513, Los Angeles, California, 90031-0513, telephone 323-201-7147. All correspondence can be sent The Wapshott Press, PO Box 31513, LA CA 90031-0513. Visit our website at www.WapshottPress.com This work is copyright © 2016 by Storylandia. The Wapshott Journal of Fiction, Los Angeles, California. Copyright © 2016 Arthur Davis and is reprinted here with the copyright owner's permission.

Storylandia is always seeking quality original short stories, novelettes, and novellas. Please have a look at our submission guidelines at www.Storylandia.WapshottPress.com or email the editor at editor@wapshottpress.com

Many thanks to editor William Akin for the proofread.

Cover: Catacombes de Paris

I Have Become the Leopard was published in "Bewildering Stories," December 2012

Dining with the Devil was published in "Allegory," May 2013

The Cracked Goblet was published in "efiction/Heater," January 2014

A Sly and Knowing Grin was published in "Tales to Terrify" podcast, April 2014

The Man from Lahr was published in "Menacing Hedges," October 2014

The Unwelcome Guest was published in "Liquid Imagination," May 2015

Storylandia

The Wapshott Journal of Fiction

Founded in 2009

Issue 17, Winter 2016

Edited by Ginger Mayerson

Table of Contents

Collected Stories
by Arthur Davis

Collected Stories

by

Arthur Davis

The Man from Lahr

The small man standing in the doorway to my office could have been anybody lost in the maze of corridors that snaked through the medical building. A heavy, nondescript dark blue suit of unrecognizable style draped from his shoulders. A small rumpled brown bag about the size of a shoebox was nestled under his right arm.

"My name is Berger. Alfred Berger." The accent was middle European. A coarse mix of German and French. He was trying to stand up straight, possibly to give an impression other than the truth of his probable seventy years.

"I'm sorry," I said, straightening up my desk. "If you want an appointment, you'll have to speak to my secretary tomorrow."

He leaned against the doorframe. "Tomorrow may be too late, sir."

I glanced at my watch. "Well, if it's an emergency, Dr. Shelton Withers on the fourth floor works late on Thursday."

Berger took in the citations, diplomas, and awards, the family pictures on the desk and along the sideboard, and the rows of medical texts. "I came to see you."

"I'm really sorry," I said folding some reports

into my case, "but I'm late as it is." Helen was going to roast me alive. We were supposed to watch the second Kennedy-Nixon debate together. Having missed the first, which had already galvanized the nation and more than likely changed the history of politics, missing the second would be socially inexcusable.

Berger removed the package from under his right arm and held it out to me. "Please Dr. Russell. It's very urgent."

A friend in medical school once asked why I chose psychiatry. The answer came easily. It always had. I explained that I didn't want to look at parts of a person, some viral assault, or hemorrhage or aftermath of a car crash. I wanted to ask him about why he wanted to leave his wife, take drugs, or why she wanted to end her life.

We were having a small dinner party and then watching the debate. "Mr...."

"Berger," he said taking a cautious step forward. "Alfred Berger."

"Yes, well, Mr. Berger," I said dropping the folder on my desk. "If you can tell your story in five minutes, what's on your mind?"

"Do you believe in magic?"

"I believe in the possibility of God, the necessity of miracles, the value of psychotherapy, and the predictability of my wife's anger when I promise to be home and I'm not."

Berger didn't remove his overcoat and looked like he was born in his hat. He set the brown bag on my marble coffee table and pulled down the wrapper revealing the metallic top of a squat, clear glass jar about ten inches tall. Half a dozen holes were punched in the tin cap. He carefully lifted it from the bag and set in it the center of the table.

At first, I thought it contained the figure of a man. I was wrong. It was a man. He was bracing himself with both hands against the sides of the bottle and staring directly at me. He appeared disoriented. I quickly recalled my training and the frequency with which we can be overcome with collective hallucinations.

"He brought me to you."

"What is it?"

He was surprised. "What does it look like?"

"I'm afraid I have no idea."

"I was hopeful you would."

There was no way to be graceful, so I acted more curious than dumbstruck. "Where did you get it?"

Berger removed the lid. The object—the man—in the container looked up but made no effort to move. "I don't know his name. I don't know much about him at all."

"But you know he wanted to see me?"

"Maybe I should begin at the beginning."

I picked up the phone and dialed. There was a signal I had worked out with Helen that gave notice that either I was in the midst of an emergency or she would have to trust me. I said. "There is a situation I need to resolve." I had repeated that phrase twice before in my eighteen years in practice. Once when a patient confessed to having murdered his brother. But I never said it with more conviction than on this cold, windswept March evening.

"I arrived early this morning from Germany. I was a professor in the public school. I taught French and English. I have some family here. I wanted to see America."

"Are you ill?"

"No. I lived in my village for sixty-eight years. My cousin, who is a pharmacist in the hospital where you work, told me to contact you."

"You showed this to him and he suggested you see me?"

The animation in the bottle moved his head about, scanning my office.

"No. I asked him which doctor in the hospital he trusted most."

"But you wouldn't give me his name."

"It's hardly important now."

"I agree, Mr. Berger," I said.

"He is very real. He is just a man smaller than you or I. You must believe that what I have brought you is real."

Berger didn't evince symptoms of classical depression, exhibited no motor agitation, panic or anxiety attack. He was a tired old man on a mission and seemed to understand that it would be difficult for me to accept that simplicity. Berger extended his hand into the bottle and lifted the man out and set him on the marble table.

Nothing in my career could have prepared me for this other than my high school biology teacher, Ms. Ferraro, a taskmaster who demanded that, "a scientist should never be indifferent to possibilities."

"I was shocked the first time I saw him too."

"Which was?"

"Yesterday afternoon." Berger carefully brought the jar onto his lap as though it was as rare as the miracle he had brought me.

For some reason I thought that, this man, this creature, was connected by some magic to Berger. That they had been together for some time and that their allegiance should not be questioned.

"And yet he makes no attempt to run or hide."

"Does that surprise you?"

"It would be better for purposes of clarity and expediency, Mr. Berger, if you spent more time explaining how you came upon this man than trying to provoke my responses." I was overcome with uncertainty and responsibility.

"I just thought you would be more surprised."

"Where did you find him?" I was going to ask him where he had gotten him, as if Berger had stolen him from his rightful owner, though the thought of this creature existing, and belonging to anybody, was almost as difficult to conceive as the aberration itself.

"I'd rather not tell you now."

"Not before you hear what I have to say."

"Yes."

"Me being the most trustworthy man your cousin could think of without knowing why you were asking him such a question?"

"I am not as bright as you, doctor, but that does not make me a fool."

"In this country, you might have been better served by asking your cousin which attorney he would trust."

"In my country, people put their faith in physicians."

I got up and locked the door to my office. I was disturbed by the possibility of what Berger might have done to this creature to ensure such constrained behavior. And yet I was impressed with this man's composure and determination, his concern and obvious compassion for his ward.

"You must tell me how you came upon this man. The truth if you want my help."

That's when I learned of Lahr, a small town

south of Baden Baden on the fringe of the Black Forest between France and Germany. His family was originally from Augsburg in southwest Germany near Munich before moving to Lahr when Berger was a child. The name Berger, as it turns out, was a convenient abbreviation of his real name that he preferred not to divulge. His story was as uncomplicated as his journey. His wife passed away two years ago. He had been forced into retirement the following year. With a small pension and a son in England, he wanted to do something with the rest of his life.

"I left my village this morning before it was light. I took a train to Baden Baden, and then one to Frankfort. Then a plane from Frankfort to New York."

"When did you land in New York?"

"Two hours ago."

"Can I get you anything, Mr. Berger?"

He glanced down at the creature on the table. "What are we going to do?"

"You mentioned something about magic."

"Magic. Yes. I didn't believe it, but this day I do. If it weren't for him, I would have never made this trip."

"Who is he?"

"I do not know."

"Then where did he come from?"

"I don't know that either."

"Mr. Berger, I am trying to work this through with you. Please, concentrate." I was going through periods of belief and denial. As soon as I took my eyes from the little man, I thought I was in the middle of a grotesque hoax. The moment I returned to him, I knew I was witness to what might be one of God's great miracles. "Where did you first see this man?"

Suddenly the man began to move. Berger and I

stopped talking. The little man walked to the edge of the coffee table closest to me and stopped. He looked down at the floor and my feet below. He looked up directly at me. I could make out his eyes, his expression, which looked distressed, not frightened or fearful. I couldn't help wonder if the trip hadn't caused him some kind of internal injury, or removing him from his land, his home, might not throw him into a deep depression.

He turned from me and began to walk the perimeter of the table. His gait and balance seemed quite normal. Why hadn't he spoken, or made some kind of noise or gesture? Where were his parents? His family and children?

There had to be others. A world beyond imagination. A refugee from a nation Alfred Berger had stumbled upon. I was certain that this association was fairly new. Otherwise the temptation to speak to someone he trusted in his or neighboring villages might have been too strong to overcome.

What would P.T. Barnum make of this phenomenon? Whatever man could not understand he distrusted, and all too often wanted to destroy or steal for his own selfish gains.

This was no pigmy, no dwarf, or stunted midget. This was a biological phenomenon of the first order. A fully developed man only four or so inches tall with perfectly proportional features that had yet to acquit his intellectual capacities.

"Alfred," I said, leaning forward to press the point, "please, tell me where you met him. And, is he aware of what we are saying?"

"His name is Lobal. I call him that. It was my great grandfather's nickname. I don't believe he understands. I tried to speak to him several times."

There was also an anguish wrapped about what he had brought me. Alfred knew he had been given something rare. Something beyond his rationale or command. He needed help. Rather than trust who he knew, he would trust his instincts. I did not want to let him down. In such a short period of time, I felt as though both Lobal and Alfred had become my responsibility. "Alfred, is there some reason why you don't want to tell me where and how you found him?"

He stared over my shoulder to the night and the street outside, squinting briefly as though trying to span the breadth of water and land that separated him from his native village. Where he was safe and secure. Where he had been overcome with wanderlust at an advanced age, when most men were settling their affairs.

"Yesterday, the day before I left," he began in English that was less than natural. "I visited the grave of my wife. My Myiah. I fell to my knees and wept. I told her I wanted to do her memory justice. She loved me. She was the only person who believed in me, who did not judge me by my faults and weaknesses. She saw me as strong and wise. She was never far from my side. She was my life."

The image of Helen giving birth to our first child materialized. It was as clear as the day it happened. The thought of not being with this woman was too impossible to bear. I watched the small man take his place in the middle of the coffee table next to the humidor as Berger returned to the story.

"I confessed that I could not make the trip. That I was going to return the ticket I had purchased. That was my third trip to my Myiah's grave in a week. When I removed my hands from my face and opened my eyes, I noticed a small figure. At first, I thought it was a salamander or twig lying on her grave. It was Lobal. He was sleeping on the top of the mound of earth."

"Sleeping?"

"I don't know what else to call it. He was wearing exactly what he is in now. He was lying on his side. I think his eyes were closed. At first, I did not notice him. It was only when I began to pray, to talk to Myiah aloud that he rose to his feet. He did not try to flee or hide. He just turned in my direction and looked up."

"Quite remarkable." Helen asked me not to use that expression. It was trite, too cumbersome for a natural response. It was pretentious. I caught myself as I was about to repeat the exclamation.

I never imagined myself a candidate for notoriety or celebrity, but the story that would be told of this small woodsman would be front page in every city and hamlet in the civilized world. What was going to happen to Alfred Berger and his trusted physician, Warren Russell, would rewrite history. There was no denying the thrill that rose within me.

"How do you communicate with him?"

"I'm not sure I do. He is not frightened of me. He did not resist when I picked him up from the cemetery. I gave him food and water. He points to his mouth when he wants either. He is not frightened of me and I have tried to be as gentle with him as I would be with a child."

"Who else knows about him?"

"No one."

"You've taken a great risk coming here."

Berger tightened his body, a characteristic I knew which often prefaced an announcement. A declaration. "Yes. But I think I have chosen wisely."

The phone rang. It was Helen. More concerned than displeased with the outcome of the evening. She had told the company that it was an emergency at the hospital. An hour had passed. She simply wanted to know if I would be able to join them for coffee. "I'm fine, I'm sorry I can't be with you."

"You're a lucky man," he said.

"Alfred, what do you want me to do?"

Without hesitation, as though he was as perplexed with his ward, "I don't know."

Alfred Berger, a brave, lonesome man taking his life in his hands, leaving his home—homeland—comes upon this man, a talisman—and makes it his mission to get them both to the new world. Quite possibly without this creature, Alfred might have backed out of his commitment. But where did the man come from? His health and safety were utmost in my mind. I would have to call two people. The head of psychiatry and internal medicine at the hospital. I would ask them here. This evening. To drop whatever they were doing and come to my office.

"Do you want me to keep him overnight?"

"I hadn't thought about that."

"Is he safe with your cousin?"

"They were very upset with me for leaving as soon as I arrived."

"Did they say anything about what was in the brown bag?"

"There was some discussion. I know they were curious."

I reached out my hand, slowly, as if I were approaching any strange animal. The small man moved toward my hand. His gait was less steady now. I was impressed and smiled broadly. I bent down, closer. "Hello."

"I tried to speak to him, in several languages," Berger said. "He did not answer me."

The face on the small man was clear. It was almost handsome. There was a resemblance I could not yet associate. He looked questioningly at me then turned to Alfred and the glass jar that had been his home.

"Is it dangerous to keep him?"

"In your cousin's home? Yes. I believe so."

The man was wearing a coarse village shirt, pants, and a torn heavy green jacket. His shoes were too small to identify. He turned and leaned weakly against the lip of the ashtray.

"We have to be very careful."

"We know nothing about him. Where he came from. What might frighten him or cause him harm or illness?"

"Nothing frightens him." Berger said as if he were defending his own honor and reputation.

"We don't know that. He may be a very brave man, but he's still," I caught himself, "human."

Berger nodded. It was obvious the man was exhausted.

"We don't know where he comes from or what might traumatize him. If we can't care and feed him he will not survive."

This alarmed Berger. The first thing that had to be done was to provide Lobal with a safe, clean environment, try and establish a baseline for his vital signs and communicate with the little man. A linguist familiar with Central European languages would be helpful to uncover the truth of the riddle. I knew such a scholar.

"I'll make some calls. We shouldn't wait until morning," I said knowing my first call would be to my lawyer. I was more concerned with the possibility that, fearful of spreading disease and, for political and scientific reasons, the authorities would have reason to quarantine the little man. I picked up the receiver and began to dial just as Lobal fell against the ashtray.

"What's wrong?"

I was immediately alarmed. "I'm not sure."

Being carried around in a glass jar for twelve hours would disorient anybody. I was more assured when Lobal walked around the perimeter of the table. And yet even that outing didn't maintain a perfect line edge to edge. There was no sign of distress, except the man's problem holding his head erect. It began moments ago and now it had become more obvious. Had there been cervical damage? Internal damage? Was Lobal in pulmonary distress? I couldn't even imagine the size of the organs necessary to sustain him.

"We have to do something."

"Alfred, do you think he needs fluids... to eat?"

"No. I gave him water and a small piece of bread before I left my cousins. They thought I was unpacking."

"Could he be injured?"

"I don't know. He was fine when we left," Alfred said reaching out to Lobal. He gently touched the side of the little man.

Lobal managed to turn his head to Alfred then lifted his right arm, and tried to motion, to wave, to implore, to beckon. It was impossible to be certain of the reason for the gesture. I got on my hands and knees at the side of the table. The perspective from this angle was quite different. Lobal took on a more human form.

There were black dots for eyes, threads for

fingers, and a faint smudge on his head where hair should be. He was proportionally perfect. And he reminded me of what a nascent Alfred Berger might have looked like. It was not important to bring this up now but the similarity was startlingly obvious. I didn't understand the connection or coincidence. But it was obvious that Lobal was gravely ill. I leaned over and called Shelton Withers. Withers had specialized in internal medicine before he changed to psychiatry. The line rang. The answering service interrupted. I dropped the phone back in the receiver.

Lobal was now resting on his back. Alfred was on his knees at his side. "What have I done?"

Lobal's chest heaved. He was looking directly up at the ceiling.

"I wish we could speak to him."

Alfred said, "I tried that all night. I wanted him to talk. When I first saw him, I couldn't believe my eyes. He simply looked at me. He seemed to trust me. Right next to my wife. As though she had given him to me from her grave. An omen, a talisman to keep me safe on my journey."

A knock on the door. "What is it?"

"Cleaning service."

"Not now," I barked. "Please, come back later."

"He's going to die."

"We can't let him die," I insisted, as though I was losing part of myself. I wanted Helen to see this. To experience what I had been given. Now, wasted. All wasted.

What must have gone through Lobal's mind? What brought him to the grave of Myiah Berger? How did he survive the trip?

Lobal's breathing became progressively labored. The possibility of a natural death crossed my mind. Had he already lived out his life; had his experiences, his excesses and exuberance, his determination and discovery? Had he given the world a family, a generation? Perhaps he was driven to Myiah's grave where he clung, as his own resting place and symbolically marking the end of Berger's life.

"Doctor Russell!"

Lobal glanced from side to side, and tugged at his collar. Not in a violent, clutching movement, but as someone would to temporarily relieve themselves.

"I don't believe we can do anything, Alfred."

Alfred extended his index finger to the little man. Lobal struggled to respond, to raise his arms. The connection to Alfred was obvious.

I believed in many things. My training and perspective had served Ms. Ferraro's dictum. I questioned much, and let possibilities abound. Few in life realized the importance of openness and a willingness to believe in what you have no training or experience to accept.

"Look," Alfred said.

Lobal turned his head to Alfred. It took a tremendous effort. "I think he's trying to speak," I said.

"I shouldn't have taken him with me."

"Would you have come without him?"

"Nothing is worth this. Look. He is dying," Alfred said bitterly. Tears heaving down his face. "And for what. For me?"

Alfred pushed the ashtray away. Lobal's arms and legs were still. I gently touched the man's chest. I believed Lobal was in cardiac distress. I also believed that the sensation recorded across the tip of my finger was unlike any I had experienced. It was warm, soothing, as a balm would offer relief to the suffering or afflicted.

"Alfred, I think he was ill before he got here. He might have been ill when you found him." I knew the words of a doctor meant everything to a layman, especially a man who was going to feel guilty for the death of this talisman that enabled him to break away from his past and give him a better life in the future.

He was surprised. "You believe that?"

"You fed and comforted him. You tended him as no one else would. If anything, you may have prolonged his life. You must believe that you befriended him. Gave him reason for hope, as he befriended you and made your journey possible."

Both men sat silent vigil for another few minutes before Alfred spoke. "I don't think he's breathing."

Remembering all too late, I went to my desk and got a magnifying glass, a present from an opera singer who had been an early patient of mine. I leaned over Lobal and for the first time could see his face clearly. His eyes were closed. The resemblance to Alfred Berger was now startling. And, though he had indeed just passed away, his body looked like it was already decomposing. His face wrinkled and the crest of his chest hollowed.

I thought of running down the hall for a camera to authenticate what I was observing. Make a record of what may never be seen again. Instead, I decided not do anything.

"Alfred, I think your friend is dead."

Alfred looked lost, defeated. He returned to his chair. He searched the office and himself for an answer. "You said he looked like me."

"Like you?"

"I thought he did too. On the plane, I looked

into the container. I thought there were some similarities, as a younger man, of course. But I think you were right. He was already quite ill."

The body of the small man had crumbled in upon itself. His remains were so desiccated that to move what was left would be to destroy what remained, the configuration of a human being that might have been some recent mutation, or a legacy from man's past.

"What am I to do?"

"Take advantage of what your friend has given you. He enabled you to start your life again. That's a legacy you must fulfill."

"I don't understand."

"I don't think I do entirely either," I said, trying not to unconsciously slip back into my role as therapist. "You needed help and your prayers were answered. We cannot question the form or substance of that intervention. We can only accept it and appreciate it for what it was and hope that we do it honor with the rest of our lives."

"You sound like the priest in my village."

"I will never be the same because of your trust in me, Alfred."

"And he trusted me," Berger said without looking at the table. "I feel responsible for him."

"Your friendship may have given Lobal more life than he might otherwise have had. Again, I suspect he was gravely ill when you found him."

Berger went on about his past and the promise of his future without taking his eyes from the small figure on the table. Both of us were mindful of what we would have given to reverse time, to bring Lobal back, to keep him alive.

"When you came into my office and I insisted

that you call my secretary for an appointment..."

"Yes."

"And you said, 'tomorrow may be too late...'"

"I think I knew from the beginning."

"That he was dying?"

"That the magic wouldn't last."

Alfred Berger confessed much to me that night. We shook hands, embraced, and parted. He put the remains of his friend back into the glass jar. I never asked him what he was going to do with it. I knew that the story that began in a small German village ended in my office without scientific inquiry. Simply, two men mourning a terrible, unfortunate fate.

In the last two hours, my life had changed. I felt more like the man I was in the beginning. When I had started my medical practice. When I met Helen. When life offered a banquet of possibilities. I looked forward to getting home.

It was close to midnight when I left my office. I called my wife and told her that I was on my way. As I locked my office for the night, I glanced at the marble table that had once held something so wonderful and remarkable.

It would remain a secret. It would inhabit a private place in my heart, and in the heart of his companion, Lobal would remain alive forever.

Dining with the Devil

Daniel Sullivan tightened the braided black and red silk cord around his waist and smoothed over the apron it was holding in place. Ricardo had repeatedly cautioned him that casual appearance compromised presentation, and the restaurant business was first about presentation, then cuisine. The imposing owner and chef's word was absolute. His impeccable standards had propelled, in only two years, Le Refuge Rouge to become one of the most sought after cafés along New York's fabled Madison Avenue.

Daniel chastised himself for his sloppiness and walked over to the new patron who had just been seated at table thirteen. "Good afternoon sir, and welcome to Le Refuge Rouge. Would you care for a drink?"

"No," the man answered without looking up.

The man at table six finally signaled for a check. Daniel glanced at his watch. Two hours to eat a spinach salad.

"I will have an order of our warm biscuits and sparkling water brought to your table."

"That's not necessary."

Daniel promptly asked, "Then may I suggest

our specials?"

"I know what I want."

The man's voice was hollow, yet deep and commanding. The menu and wine list went untouched at the far side of his table. "What would you like?"

"I want the soul of man."

Daniel's pen paused over the order pad. "Excuse me?"

"The soul of man. You do have that here, don't you?"

Daniel looked around the reserved confines of Le Refuge Rouge, hoping that the request went unnoticed. The location of the tables at the exclusive Upper East Side restaurant were designed to insure unaccustomed privacy and, with luncheon entrees running from seventy-five to over a hundred dollars, the sanctuary had become a haven for hedge fund managers, investment bankers, industrialists, fawning politicians, ladies who lunched and, especially in this city, its share of crazies. You just had to know how to handle them.

"We have what's on the menu, sir," Daniel said, first noticing that the man was wearing a long black, silk cape. "The fresh Chilean sea bass is delicious, or you can have the black skillet mussels as an appetizer or main dish. The house specials are foie gras terrine with pepper gelee, potato 'risotto,' or beef fillet in red wine and shallot sauce."

The man looked up and stared into Daniel's unsure eyes. The skin covering his face was stretched taught over his bones revealing a harsh angularity that radiated indifference. "You do prepare specials? I mean, for some particular guests you will create something quite original, wouldn't you?"

"Yes," Daniel said.

"Then be good enough to do as I asked."

Daniel, now visibly shaken, wrote down "One Soul" and marched back into the kitchen.

"Who's the ghoul at table thirteen?" Katie asked and rushed by with two steaming bowls of French onion soup on her serving tray.

Daniel fastened the order to the metal spring clasp over the chef's station and went about his business, which included managing seven of the other twenty-eight tables. By the time he filled his tray again with food for the three businessmen squabbling discreetly at table eighteen, he hoped table thirteen would be abandoned.

He delivered two grilled guinea hen paillards with foie gras mousse to the young couple at table fifteen and gave a check to the two women who had just polished off their warm, sticky toffee puddings at number ten and could feel two eyes burning a hole in the back of his head.

He turned and moved toward thirteen. "Yes, sir?"

"I don't like to wait."

Daniel tried not to look directly into the man's eyes. "I gave your order directly to our chef."

"Then I am certain he will attend to it immediately," the man said, turning his attention to the beautiful blonde sitting alone at the far side of the restaurant.

Daniel checked his wristwatch. Only an hour left and he would be off to his graduate acting workshop at New York University's prestigious Cunningham Film Institute with a story no one would believe. He watched Katie cross to the single man at table nine gulping down his dessert while skimming through *The Wall Street Journal*.

Daniel tightened his belt, recalling his penchant for indulging in the unsold desserts, especially Ricardo's famously infamous chocolate tart with bittersweet caramelized orange peel, also one of Katie's favorites. In the three weeks since she'd started, they'd shared many culinary indecencies in addition to a love of opera, ballet, early Woody Allen movies, and the Marx brothers.

A sickening feeling welled up in his stomach. First, the crazy lady at table ten last Monday loudly insisting that the butter used by Le Refuge Rouge was really margarine, as if Ricardo would ever permit such poison in the back door, and now Count Dracula wanted a soul food special.

Daniel thought to ask if he wanted the soul rare, medium, or well done. He returned to table thirteen. "I'm sorry sir; we're fresh out of soul."

Daniel finally noticed the man's large hands. They were unusually smooth, long, and narrow. His fingernails were manicured and polished, practically cut to a point. They were the hands of a man who had never raised anything more substantial than an idea. Daniel guessed the man was about fifty, maybe a few years, or a few hundred years, older.

"I don't think you understood my request, young man," the man said, standing to the full measure of his six-foot, seven-inch frame. Customers nearby stopped eating and gaped at the man's towering dark presence. "I didn't ask if you had any. I don't care whether you do or you do not. That's of little consequence to me. I ordered a very special dish. Where or how you collect the ingredients is your chef's concern, though it is my belief that if you presented my request to him, I will be satisfied with the outcome of his efforts."

Daniel was caught by the man's hand on his

shoulder. Those long delicate fingers dug into his shirt until he winced. "Let me check our stock again."

"Daniel, do not check the stock. Do as I instructed. That is all I require from you."

Daniel was startled that the man knew his name or that Ricardo might know how to prepare such a dish. He pulled away. "My apologies. I'll see to it immediately, sir," he said, wrote up another order slip, and handed it directly to Ricardo, something usually frowned upon in this class of kitchen.

"I don't need two," he said, nodding to Daniel, and slowly walked to the back of the kitchen.

The pain in Daniel's shoulder had worked its way into his back. Sweat slicked his face. Hadn't anybody out there noticed the monster in the black cape, black suit, and red satin tie with the slick black hair and blood stained eyes? Oh my God, the man has red eyes, Daniel suddenly realized.

"You look sick," Katie mentioned, washing her hands.

"A bit of a problem at thirteen."

"He's very handsome. Is he one of your actor friends come in for a handout?" she winked.

The moment he returned to the dining room the man at thirteen waved him over. After a while he looked up, his faint grin collapsing into frozen resolve, "Young man, either I have the soul of a man on my table in five minutes or I'll take yours. And when I'm finished I will take the soul of your little girlfriend over there. I believe her name is Katie."

The pain in his shoulder grew with every breath, as if the man's fingers were embedded in his flesh. Now, the man threatened him and Katie. He should call the police. Ricardo had to be told. This was no longer a joke or the whim of a madman.

Daniel walked cautiously over to the preparation counter and spotted an oversized dish with steam bubbling fanatically out of a frothy brown and gray mass he had never encountered in his three years of waiting tables, from the smallest coffee shop to this retreat. It looked like squashed sweetbread and smelled quite foul. For a second, he thought he saw something undulate between the crevasses of the grapefruit size mass. There were no vegetables or garnish.

"Use your side towel," Ricardo instructed, standing on the other side of the counter. "And do not speak to him after you serve it. Just walk away."

"Are you all right?"

"Daniel, do exactly as I say, now. Just go do it," Ricardo said, and began to wash his hands with disinfectant.

He grabbed the side towel folded on his apron and pinched his hand around the lip of the plate. It was searing, scalding hot. Hotter than any dish he had ever felt. He quickly doubled the towel over once, then again before grasping the scorching plate. He walked through the swinging doors as if he was carrying his own heart in his hands. He gently set down the plate and, without thinking about Ricardo's instructions, asked the man if there would be anything else.

"Send a bottle of Château Lafite Rothschild 1982 to that table," he said, nodding toward the blonde woman sitting alone by the window.

It was not uncommon for him to present a bottle of wine or Champagne, though hardly one so expensive, to a beautiful woman. Invariably the man would make his presence known in his own time. Once he had seen Katie deliver a fine Riesling to a woman from another woman. He couldn't recall how that offering played out.

Two older, elegantly dressed women came into the restaurant. They were seated near the front window after being reassured by the maître d' that Le Refuge Rouge was still serving lunch. Both glanced over at the man in the cape. Daniel wanted to warn them off as he prayed for the woman about to be given the gift of an '82 Lafite.

He wished he had stayed in bed this one chill, overcast March day, heeding his horoscope's warning that he would be better served "avoiding responsibility rather than exposing himself to great risk."

The man had not picked up a spoon or added seasoning. His hands rested on the table, not a hint of movement or intent. He was staring down into the still roiling mass. Daniel checked the status of his other tables and walked into the kitchen. It was just three o'clock. Katie and the two other waiters were checking their final orders.

Ricardo stood alone going over the evening menu when Daniel approached. "I know who he is," Ricardo said before Daniel could speak. "That's all you have to know."

"Is he a friend?"

"Who he is doesn't concern you. Or anybody."

Daniel walked out to the back alley still stinging from Ricardo's tone. Katie was standing next to the four-story brick building, taking her second drag. After smoking two packs a day for eight years, the twenty-six year old ex-artist and dancer from Helena, Montana, had worked herself down to half a pack a day. She quickly crushed out the embers against the side of the building.

Daniel thought she was pretty and sexy, and was completely distrustful of her past. Kenny, one of the waiters, claimed she had been a back-up singer with a rock group in Los Angeles. To Daniel, that meant drugs, alcohol, and having sex with every man with an instrument, musical or not. He knew his assessment was harsh, but he couldn't help himself. He was no prig, nor was he particularly accepting of every lifestyle.

"You look like you've got yourself a winner there."

"You've noticed."

"Everyone has."

"So, what do you think I should charge him for a human soul?"

Her eyes widened with surprise. "He ordered what?"

"A human soul."

A shudder swept through her body. She wrapped herself in her own arms, wishing they belonged to Daniel. "That's disgusting."

"Evil. I think."

"Did you ask Ricardo?" Katie asked, suddenly aware she was fantasizing about what Daniel looked like under his apron. If she could only be certain he was as curious about her as she was about him.

"I did."

"What did he say?"

"He said he would take care of it, and not to return to thirteen until the guy left."

"He shouldn't be here, whoever he is. Look at him, sucking up every last drop of that slop like an animal over its prey. What is that shit, anyway?"

Daniel wanted to call the police, or at least warn Katie. How could he tell her about the man's threat? He should have told Ricardo. That was a mistake.

"The guy's straight out of a 1950s horror flick."

"Ricardo knows who he is and he's frightened, and I've seen him scream obscenities in the face of hardened city health inspectors. The guy would stare down the devil if he had to."

Moreover, this was no 50s horror flick. He had a half hour left on his shift. He asked Kenny if he could cover his tables if he left early. Kenny shrugged his agreement knowing that Daniel must have first cleared the request with Ricardo. Daniel dashed into the back, changed into his street clothes, and was secluded in a delicatessen across the street when the man with the cape came out of Le Refuge Rouge a half hour later.

The man glanced up and down Madison Avenue. His cape flapped wildly in the breeze. He half expected the guy to spread his cape and fly away. Instead, he removed a cigarette from a silver case, lit it, looked up directly into the late afternoon mist, and started walking. There was a grace, a slow fluidity about him, as if he were being whisked along by an unseen force.

Women turned appreciatively as he walked by. Daniel glanced down at his watch again. He had to get down to class. His instructor was as insistent on punctuality as performance. Then, just as he decided to wait another few minutes before rushing to the subway, the man turned directly toward him.

A city bus passed in front of him and blocked out the visage of the man's glare. When the light changed and the bus moved on, the man was no longer in sight. Daniel looked up and down Madison Avenue and peered into a few of the retail shops. He went back into the restaurant and found Ricardo standing alone in the back alley where he had been talking to Katie. He assumed she had already left for her other job.

"There is a malevolence about him."

Ricardo thought for a while. "You may be right."

"What did you serve him?"

The chef was half a foot taller, half a hundred pounds heavier, and half a life older than Daniel. He had a reputation for being uncompromising with his standards and staff. "You don't want to know too much."

"Why? What would happen if I knew?" Daniel offered, the actor in him crying out with curiosity, for answers, for a way to separate himself from the rest of the flock that got parts he might have earned.

"You could go to sleep with the curse of his glare in your memory and wake up in the middle of the night with his thoughts corrupting your heart."

"Is that what he's done to you?"

"It doesn't matter. He's gone."

"Ricardo, what's he done to you?"

"He has done everything to me," he said, his hands covering his face in despair. "He has left me with little else other than my craft which, strangely enough, also serves his needs from time to time. He has taken everything that is dear to me including my father and sister, as well as the spirit of my mother."

Daniel was jarred by the image of this large powerful man being reduced to such a state. "How?"

"Please."

"He sat at my table and looked into my eyes like he knew what I was thinking and where I would hide if he ever wanted to find me. He ordered the soul of man and got his dish and spoke to me as though if I did not do as he wished he would reach into my chest and squeeze the life out of my heart."

Ricardo nodded. "Be thankful if that's all he takes."

"What do you mean?"

Ricardo liked Daniel. The boy gave him an honest day's work, and had no attitude or agenda. He was fair to a fault and minded his own business. "It doesn't matter."

"He said he had asked for that dish before."

"He has been at my doorstep once a year wherever I've worked."

"Ricardo, please, who is he?"

"You do not understand."

"Who is he?"

"You may pay a high price for your curiosity."

"Please."

"Then I will. If only to have you stop questioning me."

"And, believe me that whatever you tell me will stay with me and die with me." It was a line in the play Daniel was rehearsing, though he meant every word of it.

"Be careful what pledges you make Daniel. What you take to the grave may visit you long after you've drawn your last breath. "

"I'm listening."

"I will swear on the grave of my father and sister that this man is the Prince of Darkness."

"I'm listening." Daniel said, already accepting that unreality.

"There is little to tell besides the truth, and that's impossible to believe," Ricardo began. "I come from a small village in northeast Spain near the French border. It's not noteworthy in any other sense except for the bond of our people and their proud heritage. My father was a town clerk. A civil servant. My mother, bless her soul, gave birth to four children. I was the last. A terrible pestilence swept through our valley two years after I was born, ravaging men and women, but mostly the very young. Both my older brothers died in the scourge. I survived, along with my sister."

"I'm sorry."

"He visited my parents some years later. He came into our home one night and told them who he was and what he had come for. They were to do his bidding, when and if he asked, for a period of one year. There was no surprise in their eyes, only disappointment that their home had been chosen in order that my village would be spared. He had visited other houses over the years since our village sprang from the mountain landscape. He had cursed us forever. No family went untouched by his cruelty."

Ricardo's gestures, his words, were anguished. Daniel suddenly had no interest in knowing the tale that was unfolding in front of him. But it was already too late. It was as if he were looking at a train wreck that couldn't be stopped and he was part of that oncoming disaster.

"I was still too young to understand the custom that had plagued my village and my parents and the homes of their parents, relatives, and friends for generations back, since the darkest part of Europe's Dark Ages. There were no radios or newspapers to expose this evil, no science to delve into its corrupting power, no police, and no government strong enough to protect them from this inhuman incarnation.

"But my father hesitated, and in that one tragic moment, this man who goes by no name swept his hand out like a giant scythe and in that gesture took the last breath from my little sister's lungs. My mother fell to her dying side, my father cried out in rage and fury. The arm my father raised against this man was cut from his shoulder in a flash. Severed clean by the sword his fingers became. They reached out and just cut off his arm to the shoulder. My father bled to death crying in the arms of my mother and his only surviving child.

"After some time his fury subsided, though not until his breath charred the wooden walls of our home. He demanded that the soul of a man be prepared for him every year in retribution for the insult that had been hurled against him by my father. It was also a lesson for our village which had been visited by him, as I said, since as long as anyone could recall."

"My God."

"If only there was one Daniel, if only there was one."

"What about your family?"

"He gave my mother the recipe and she pledged she would prepare it until her son was old enough to carry on with his command, which is what I do each and every year. And whenever he shows up, I am reminded of my doomed sister and the anguished death cry of my father and all those damned souls who went into the night before them."

Whatever he was prepared for, this horror was beyond his imagination. From a simplistic view of good and bad, there was never a manifestation of evil. Evil in the heart of man was regrettable, terrible, not personified except in movies, theater, in books and tales parents told their children to scare them into curtailing their mischief. "That's almost impossible to believe."

"Believe what you want."

"Can I ask you where you got whatever it was you served him?"

"You can ask, of course. But I would never

reveal what I had to do to obtain such a thing."

I could not believe what I was hearing and yet, if you had been at my side and witnessed the suffering in this man's defeated face you would not doubt a word of his tale. "What about the cape? The whole getup? It all looks like it comes from central casting."

"You have it backwards. Everyone has."

"I don't understand."

"He didn't get it from central casting, as you refer to his costume. They got it from him, and over the centuries, from scattered reports from small cities and villages all over the world. That's the irony of it all. Many have seen him in his travels and those encounters, however afar, will always remain in their minds. That's what he wore thirty-seven years ago in my home. That's what he wore a hundred and thirty-seven years ago in someone else's home in another poor village in some other part of the world. That's what he will be wearing a hundred years from now in some ravaged village in Africa or India or Central America."

"Can't we do something?"

"We can call the police and they will laugh at us. We can call the newspapers but what would they investigate besides our sanity?"

"And the people of your village?"

"What do you think he would do to them and my mother who is there alone despite my wanting her to join me in America? You have seen the merest fraction of his rage. Would you be willing to expose the truth if it meant hundreds, maybe thousands would be consumed in the effort to uncover his identity, as well as every member of your family and every one of their friends?"

Daniel quickly grasped the implications of

Ricardo's warning, but persisted. "We have to do something."

"We just did," Ricardo said getting up. "We gave my mother and my village another year of life."

Daniel watched Ricardo walk back into the restaurant as Katie came out in her street clothes. "What was that all about?"

Daniel didn't know what to say. "I thought you left already?"

"No, I'm working on a catering job with Kenny this weekend for some extra loot. We just had to go over some last minute details."

"I have rehearsals Saturday and Sunday, or I'd be there too. I could use the money."

"You look like you could use a stiff drink."

"That too."

"I guess my idea about following that guy wasn't so great."

"No. You were right. I just had to come back before I went down to class. I followed him for a while until I got bored. It was nothing with nothing. And you're probably right about him being an actor."

"Are you sure?"

"Trust me Katie."

"Then was anything wrong with Ricardo?"

"No. Nothing, but do you know where he worked before he came here?"

"All over, I've heard. Rome, for a long time after he left Spain. And Madrid I think. Then Montreal, Canada. I think he was in Los Angeles for a while, God help him. He's been working here in the city for about five years now."

"I didn't know any of that."

"Ricardo is an okay guy. He's never hit on me or any of the girls, or guys for that matter."

Daniel had no intention of breaking a confidence, especially with Ricardo and most especially with this tale of tales. "I like him."

"Do you want to pick me up after the catering is over?"

Daniel wanted to. He and Katie had been growing together since he started flirting with her only weeks ago. But now, well, he was distracted. "I'll see."

"I'll let you take me home and ravish me."

All he could think of was Ricardo's mother living out every day in fear that her son might fail to provide the devil with his due. "I'll let you know tomorrow."

"What makes you think my offer is going to be there tomorrow?" Katie said, and grew angry and walked away.

Daniel replayed every word of Ricardo's story, resolved that someday he would draw upon the despair of such a character for one of his roles. Since he could do little else to relieve Ricardo's burden, perhaps honoring him by exploring the range of his suffering would make a difference. He took a deep breath and forced the image of the man from his mind.

He had never ravished a woman.

At this moment, all he wanted was to find her and tell her how pretty she was. He also wanted to check the refrigerator for any chocolate tarts with bittersweet caramelized orange peel that he could use as a peace offering to her.

He did both.

Cara's Curve

It was almost eleven. The road was streaked with black ice from the freezing afternoon rain, making the winding three-mile wooded stretch outside of Chester, Pennsylvania even more treacherous. Charles Kearny's headlights poked yellow fingers into the night.

Kearny let the steering wheel slip from his hands. The plastic wheel jerked around haphazardly. Time accelerated into uncountable moments of uncertainty. The landscape of night and steep rolling decline was split by a series of exaggerated, unstable 'S' curves where construction expediency had compromised driving safety.

He never told Cara about his driving adventures. There were so many things he had wanted to say to her. He knew she would have understood and taken him into her arms. Her warm sweet breath caressing his neck. Her words drowning out his sirens of doubt.

His right knee still ached from the fall he took two months ago at the plant. He was too proud to report to the infirmary. Even then, he had sensed a change in management. Defeat had overtaken a once proud company. The plant was closing in a month. That was the announcement they had withheld until the end of the week. Until the end of this charcoal damp day.

Production was being transferred to the upgraded Glasgow facility closer to key suppliers and a more efficient railroad terminal. A hundred and eighty-three men and women were about to lose their pride. Last year he lost his Cara who was his life, and now his job, which was all that remained of his identity and dignity.

Kearny brought the cold plastic wheel back into the palm of his right hand and eased back on the accelerator. Ahead, his lights reflected off a sign with two parallel squiggles announcing another series of unforgiving curves. A mistake here and he would slam into the revetment on his right or spill down the embankment to his left. At fifty miles per hour, there would be little left for the police to identify.

The men at the plant might consider he had lucked out. Some, like Biggs, would have no doubt that Kearny had taken his own life.

That bothered Kearny. He didn't want to be thought of as weak. What had happened to his wife was a terrible, personal tragedy. The closing of the plant was a local catastrophe. Did that justify taking such drastic action?

Biggs was a loafer, a fattened sloth of a shop steward who thought the worst of every man because of what he saw in himself. Others might suspect the truth because they knew how good a driver Kearny was and how often he took this route and indeed, how often he bragged that he had mastered it and tested the limits of the beast.

"Then what would have been Charlie Kearny's intent?" he asked himself.

The yellow probes flared back off something

hidden in the thickets ahead as he slowly slipped off the road into a fog-shrouded clearing. Water spurted from the branches and leaves under his tires. The right front tire needed to be aligned. Cara thought they should have replaced it long ago. She was right. She was invariably right.

It was a year since her heart attack. Since her lungs filled with fluids so fast, she drowned in her own essence. She was gone less than a week after she was taken away by ambulance. He sat at her bedside in the hospital, never letting go of her hand. At night when the nurses came to tell him it was time to leave, he would press his cheek against her hand and close his eyes.

Charlie opened his door. White puffs of steam jumped from his mouth into the uncertain darkness. A thick ground-fog obscured everything beyond a few yards.

He could feel his insides heave. He wanted to get out. Run somewhere. Hide. Deny himself his past and future. "I miss you honey," he sobbed.

It had been months since he'd cried over the loss of his wife of twenty-six years. Most friends predicted the union wouldn't last the wedding night. But this engaging, delicate girl with faint green eyes and dark curly hair shared, along with her new husband, the strength to work things out and not let love be distracted or compromised.

The coronal glare of his headlights reflected off the outline of a car embedded in a rage of brambles twenty yards to his right.

"Hello there," Kearny said, following the tire tracks in the wet soil. One of the headlights was on. The engine hummed on indifferently.

Kearny moved up to the side of the driver's

door. The window was open a few inches. "You all right?" he asked loudly. The figure inside remained cast in protective shadows. Kearny could see the outline of the body, the two extended arms, and the hands still clutching the steering wheel.

The reflection of the moon washed through the windshield. The man's eyes were open. He was in his mid-forties. He was staring ahead with an unbroken intensity. Charlie rapped on the window. The man in the dark green parka, thick-rimmed black glasses, and look of dismay wasn't breathing.

"I've never seen a dead man. Not up close like this. It's really crazy. You're dead and I almost killed myself. And you're still a hell of a lot better looking than fat Biggs."

Charlie opened the car door, reached into the man's pockets to find some identification. A bill from a tailor with no name at the top, for two pairs of pants.

"You killed yourself. I can tell. I read where a man can think himself to death. If you hold onto anger or hate and never let them go they feed on you until the soft, poisonous goo eats rots away your insides."

The man remained dead.

"Bad thoughts. They'll kill you as if you put a gun to your head and pulled the trigger." Charlie reached up to close the man's eyes then stopped. That's what coroners do for a living, not metalworkers. Even ex-metalworkers.

He got back into his car and found his cell. The reception was terrible. Walking around to get a better connection, he got through to the police on his third try. He mentioned there was a dead man, with an unexpected urgency.

He mused that it would have been interesting, like in those horror films, if the car and body had disappeared when he returned. Swept into the night by a ghoul or vampire or something that threaded the cracks between the pillars of reason and time.

The mud softened under foot as he retraced his steps to the side of the car. "Between the lousy connection and the asshole sergeant, let's hope they get here before morning," Kearny said, searching his pockets for a cigarette.

"My wife Cara's favorite line from a song," Charlie began, "goes: 'God is watching us from a distance.' I never appreciated it until she passed away. He is, you know. He's up there watching and caring."

Another drag on the cigarette and he could feel himself relax, or be as at ease as the situation would allow.

"So, you want to tell me what happened? What was so important that you couldn't let go of? Just between you and me. Man to man. I wouldn't tell anybody. It'll just be our secret. You can trust me. If there's one thing I can do its keep a secret. But, hey, if you don't want to talk, I'm OK with that too."

He was just about the same age as this guy. A bit thinner perhaps. They both came down this road, neither expecting their lives to be in jeopardy. Each man harboring a repellent deed or suspicion or resentment. The police were going to be here soon. Once they arrived, he would never have this opportunity again. Charlie shook his head, working through what he had to say.

"What do you think about an honest man, a regular guy, like yourself, decent in most ways, making a small mistake? One. Just once."

Charlie listened for the echo of his words. They slipped out and disappeared into the night as if they had never been said at all.

"You know. A girl, just not my wife. It happened. Nothing happened of course, but, well, it came close. She started out as a temp last summer in billing. There were some screw-ups on the Judson Industries invoices. I was working them out with her boss when she came on to me. The kid's not twenty and she's posing and smiling and nodding whenever I pass her department. And once, twice, I found myself going out of my way to pass her desk. It's as if she knew I was coming. She's bending over her desk or file cabinets each time so I could get a good look."

Charlie finally inhaled. His heart pounded. It was as if he had run a hundred yards with chains wrapped around his soul.

"I wasn't thinking straight. It never happened before. Not even a stray look. But for some reason, hey, I'm not condoning what I thought I wanted to do."

Her off-handed comment once about how he looked like he had, "strong and gentle hands," was the worst of it.

His response, what he said seemingly without hesitation, had poisoned every night he slept with Cara since the encounter in the office, and every night since she'd been taken from him. He wanted the police to come and manacle and cage him and jam a hot poker into his brain to stop the guilt.

"In the end, I wasn't worthy of her. I never realized that until tonight."

Sirens. Finally.

Charlie ran from the underbrush and into the moonlit clearing and reached for the wallet in his hip pocket as the police car pulled up. He wanted to see her face again. He couldn't wait a moment longer. The wallet was slippery against the wet of his grasp. Then he wanted to show the dead man photos of his wonderful Cara. He knew the man would understand why he was consumed with guilt if he saw how beautiful and wonderful his Cara was.

Both officers jumped out of their cruiser with guns drawn, as their sergeant cautioned might be necessary with a dead man in question, and demanded that the man first running towards them, then trying to flee, drop the small black object clutched in his hands.

Charlie finally caught a piece of their command and turned back toward the glare of the police headlights, and through the night and distance and fresh gulp of ground fog he suddenly looked as menacing as the desk Sergeant warned. Charlie's arms were outstretched in their direction, his favorite picture of his Cara out of his wallet as both officers fired. The first bullet struck him in the right side. The second caught him in the chest. The third missed completely, shattering the windshield behind him so that glass shards sprayed the man slumped at the wheel, making it look like he was in a real car accident.

The coroner arrived hours later. Both officers remarked at the inquiry that followed that they had been alerted by the desk sergeant who took the call and suspected foul play. Both officers were convinced that the man had been given ample warning and continued to behave in a "threatening and non-responsive manner."

"He turned, and looked like he was going to fire on us," the younger officer testified.

The officer's girlfriend, a pretty young blonde in her early twenties, sat shaking uncontrollably in the rear of the courtroom, fighting back the details of her boyfriends's testimony about the death of the stranger. An innocent man, she was certain, with the strong, gentle hands she had come to love.

A Sly and Knowing Grin

Kelly Christina Ramos was immediately attracted to the young man scouring the rows of old 78 rpm records in the back of Field's Antique Shop. He was tall and lean, and with a shy vulnerability about his eyes that she found hopelessly endearing.

From the dilapidated condition of his shoulder bag and frayed jacket collar, she guessed he was a student from one of the local trade schools. She stood up straight, trying to hide any remnant of her slouching posture and indiscriminate belly when the young man grabbed the elderly man standing next to him with claws that only moments ago had been long, delicate fingers, shot out a jaw of razor sharp teeth and sank them into the old man's neck.

The old man wailed, dropped his newspaper and tried to squirm free. After a few desperate attempts his arms failed, his eyes closed, and he sank down against the display case, the young man clinging to his side.

A half-dozen terrified customers ran toward the front of the store. The owner, a man well over six feet and every ounce of three hundred pounds of unflattering flesh, black jeans and filthy black shirt, stood with his arms raised in the doorway.

"No one leaves," he announced as the frenzied

band of customers spilled up against him.

"Are you crazy? Get out of the way," Kelly screamed.

The sweet old man who had graciously let her pass behind him so she could get to a stack of fine Irish linens was dying or, mercifully, had already succumbed.

Sounds of flesh being torn and bones crushed spilled from the aisle.

"We have to get out of here," one of the men said without taking his eyes off the carnage, "or we're all going to die."

"Move out of the way," another demanded, as the pileup knotted.

The manager's size and strength and resolve were more than adequate to repel the flurry of flailing fists that beat against his body.

"No. Let's try square dancing," an elderly woman offered.

"Of course," another, then another, agreed.

The owner pulled down a stack of records from a shelf overhead and slowly pumped the hand crank that spun the turntable of the antique tabletop Columbia Grafonola record player.

"Square dancing?" Kelly screamed.

She grabbed the metal waste paper basket and flung it at the window display. It bounced back and fell into a sea of rag dolls, tin toy cars, wooden duckpins, and paint-chipped dumbbells.

"I think he's stopped," the woman with wiry red hair said, standing frozen, entranced, staring at the young man. The woman was in her late fifties, slightly overweight, and in a tattered, soiled dress.

The young man rose from the other side of the counter, a chunk of flesh dangling from his jaw. His bloodstained claws reached over a wooden box stacked full with a collection of Merle Haggard favorites.

"No, he's not," a man said, out of breath from dancing with a woman who might have been his wife.

"Let us out of here," Kelly demanded.

The boy's face was splattered with an angry swath of red. His head rotated in jerking, twisting motions from side to side. His once tender, forgiving eyes bulged red and distended. He glanced around the shop again and again before dropping back down out of sight.

Another country westerny tune filled the air with a rueful whine of lost loves and endless disappointment. Only this time no one danced. The owner waved off a curious passerby trying to get into the shop and pulled down the single black shade that separated Fields Antiques from the rest of the world. What had been a space splintered with late afternoon light was suddenly cast into threatening shadows.

Kelly wanted to throw something at the owner. But she couldn't bring herself to toss any of the records that surrounded her, and had been a staple of her father's life, an obsession she willingly inherited.

Distant and distorted memories first, of her father, a short burley man who wore almost comically owlish metal rimmed eye glasses, then her mother, a resolute woman whose silhouette looked like it was the perfect female counterpart of her beloved husband, flashed brightly, then flamed out into darkness.

"Could you get me a cold glass of water?" one of the women asked.

She was only a few years older than Kelly, and held a large leather satchel under her right arm. She had been the first to press against the owner when the attack began and the first to back off at the mention of square-dancing.

"You wait right here and I'll get you a cup from my office," the owner said and bounded to the back of the shop.

"A man has been killed and you want water?"

The woman shot back angrily, "I'm thirsty. Okay?"

"What's wrong with that?" her husband demanded. "I could use something cold myself."

His wife took hold of his sleeve. "You know, Walter, maybe we could go next door to Jensen's and get a delicious scoop of ice cream? You love their Very-Cherry-Vanilla."

Without waiting for a response, the woman pulled open the front door, pushed her husband forward and they were gone. Another customer picked up his scattered groceries and rushed out behind them.

"Where did they go?" the owner asked, returning with a cup in hand.

"That's your concern?"

"You're a troublemaker, aren't you?" the owner said to Kelly, drinking the tepid water in a single gulp, and moved back to his cash register.

Of course, there was no ice water, as there would not be any ice cream, or anything else that required a compressor which, in itself, required electricity. The harsh reality was that anyone who had a generator had electricity. And you could get all the gas you needed for a generator from the millions of abandoned vehicles, which had become one of the favorite targets of the smaller patrol ships.

"What?"

"We've been warned about people like you."

"You're the one the authorities should be

warned about for not letting us out of this place."

"You can go if you want."

"Now I can go?" she sputtered, smacking the empty cup from his hand.

The owner wiped a splash of water from his face and announced, "Everyone, you can stay if you want, or go if you want to."

"And that doesn't bother you?" she asked, pointing to the young man huddled over the remains.

"Thousands of bodies in the streets and the stench in the air bothers me, lady. Children starving to death by the millions the world over bothers me. And a pack of frantic people running into the street from what's left of my store draws attention that's going to get us all killed. That bothers me even more."

Kelly had seen the bodies too. The devastation was everywhere. But this world was new to her, and she had lived so much of the last year in denial and doubt, she had a hard time coming to terms with the obvious. "But not a young man killing an old man?" she asked, in a much less demanding tone.

"Lady, we all have to make some sacrifices if we're going to survive. You know that. Everybody here knows that."

The chief resident in the upstate hospital where Kelly Ramos had spent the last few months had that same, smarmy glare, as though he knew something she didn't and, if she had, she wouldn't really have comprehended.

She had seen that sly, knowing grin on the face of the owner of the grocery store yesterday when she arrived in the city. She had seen it in men and women everywhere since being released from the hospital only days ago, and many months after the car accident that claimed her father and left her with a painful limp and in a constant state of crippling, suffocating anxiety.

A man in his early forties entered the store and acknowledged the manager with a friendly wink. "Well?"

"I have both right here," the owner said and pulled out a pair of books on model railroads from behind the counter. "Twenty-nine even." The man paid, took his parcel, but not before noticing what was going on in the aisle, shook his head in despair and left.

The owner threw the special pick-up slip into the waste paper basket that had bounced off the double-thick security window he had installed last year, and which now functioned as a sound baffle against the terrible vibration the patrol saucers made as they swept low over the neighborhood every few hours.

It had been only weeks, thirty-seven days to be exact, since heavy assault cruisers rained down destruction. There was no warning. There was no defense. There was no explanation. There were no negotiations. City after city across the globe fell to the consuming onslaught.

Kelly sneezed, reached into her bag and removed a wad of tissues, wiped her nose and recalled one the doctors, the one who had been particularly sexually aggressive towards her, warning that she might go through a period of crippling self-doubt.

"You may feel fearful, unable to make decisions, even hesitant to cross the street at times. It's common," he had said without looking up from her file. "Good luck," he added, and ushered her out of his office.

He never said how long it would last, or if she would ever recover. Maybe it would have been better to remain in the hospital, stay a few months, a few lifetimes, longer. The psychiatric wing of the hospital where she was sent to recover from her guilt and deepening depression was nothing more than a run-down clinic. But in these times, even before the invasion, much of the world was already living in a compromised state.

She was discharged, along with every ambulatory patient, weeks after the first attack. And after the military of every nation struggled to repulse the invaders and nuclear weapons were quickly abandoned as they exploded prematurely, wiping out whole military bases and nearby communities.

There was no warning, no message from the President or Pentagon announcing the invasion, or the nation's or world's plans for defense. One morning the cruisers appeared hundreds of miles overhead then descended, wiping out bridges, tunnels, and power plants; wherever infrastructure was necessary to sustain the lives of their enemy. Lines of communication were cut along with transmission lines that fed the appetite of the world economy. Every nation was struck simultaneously with the same relentless overpowering force. There was no place to turn, no place to flee. Only the certainty of death.

But life went on, almost immediately, insistently, as a collective desperation for calm quickly turned into denial and finally, acceptance. With communication nearly impossible, cities quickly fragmented into communities, communities into towns and eventually, the world settled into a frail web of isolated, ravaged villages.

After weeks of carnage came the demands, and the brutality of reprisals that were frequently used to dampen uprisings and keep the inhabitants in constant fear and subjugation.

At first Kelly wanted to call home, make contact with what remained of her family, tell them she was free, and would they forgive her for not being able to avoid the van that struck her father's side of their car. Why had God chosen to take the life of such a good man, she questioned over and over in the condemning glare of friends and family as the procession of lives moved from cemetery to the unending aftermath of tragedy.

Even with an unstable gait and some hairline scars near her forehead, she was positive she could rebuild her life, though life on earth had changed, and her planet had quickly been beaten and humiliated into submission.

The twenty-mile trek from the hospital to the city had taken her almost four days to complete. Many of the patients who started out with her were quickly spotted and cut down. Only traveling on foot and at night was possible.

The saucer-ships zigzagged across the sky, hovered, fired, left some villages untouched while decimating their neighbors, and moved on to the next cluster of humanity. A few shops were open, a few food stands, some week-old fruit, and fresh bread from people's ovens. What was most startling was not how quickly so many were overwhelmed and killed, but why so many people simply disappeared.

The owner seemed smaller, less imposing now, fumbled absently through the day's few receipts until he could no longer bear the pretty young girl's sorrowful stare. "Listen, you have to come to terms with what's happened."

Kelly hesitated until she could no longer contain both fear and the need to understand, and accept how she needed to adjust. "Which is?"

"The end of our world, our freedom, what we spent a million generations building."

"And the answer is square dancing?"

"I know. I know. It's crazy, and no one knows how that got started."

Kelly still felt unsafe, though not as confused or unconnected, as she had been for the last few days. She forced herself to trust this stranger. She had to trust someone. "So whenever one of them wants to kill one of us we all clap and dance around and that makes them go away?"

"The ones who first protested saw their towns consumed in green flashes so powerful that they melted cars and trucks where they stood. At least I have a phonograph. Mostly people just hum any tune they know. I guess it calms them down."

"I wasn't here. I really didn't know."

"Look, I'm getting out. You want to stay here you're welcome to do what you can, but I think the old man is long past dead and I don't want to be next on the kids menu."

"You're leaving?" she asked, as though she were being abandoned.

The owner finally introduced himself as Manny Perez. The shop had belonged to his brother who, she learned, was one of the first to go into the streets when the battle cruisers broke through the country's flimsy defenses. He was swept from the streets by a howling green flash. Manny pointed out where Johnny had been standing, along with a small band of frightened onlookers when they were cut down.

What had occurred in the shop was common, and tame in comparison to when one or two would attack a dozen people in malls, parking lots, or supermarkets. These outbursts were becoming more common and depraved. What was worse, the savage species could transform itself at will, without notice or warning, and so easily assume another human form.

"No one knows who they are talking to anymore. You could have been one of them. You still could be," he said, before turning away.

Kelly watched him disappear down the block. A few people were moving about, their faces fixed with fear, not looking left or right, not making eye contact. She wanted to do something. For once, take a stand and make her life count. She needed to give meaning to who she was or could possibly have been.

Two giant silver saucers glided slowly, a thousand feet above the still-smoking rubble. They were huge and had no markings. They had to be two or three times the size of the largest commercial jet, with a small raised metallic nub at the center. Kelly was transfixed by their effortless presence as they slowly glided out of sight.

Kelly couldn't recall if she had had breakfast and, for a moment, couldn't place the time of day. These blank spots, as Dr. Halpren described them, these moments of confusion and disorientation, were normal and to be expected. But they still rekindled fears that she might never return to a normal life. Then again, Kelly mused, what was the chance of that happening now that she and the rest of humanity were lost forever?

She watched three men lifting and pulling and giving hushed directions to each other amid the narrow confines of what at one time had been a jewelry store. They were scavengers, pillagers looking for valuables among the ruins of mankind.

If their efforts hadn't held her attention she never would have noticed a familiar figure moving along the street in front of a row of burned-out buildings.

The tips of her fingers tingled. Heat surged into her face. Her heart pounded as the old man shuffled along, nodding respectfully as a woman passed, going in the opposite direction. His stoop, his age, the way he held one hand clenched tightly against his ribcage eliminated any doubt. She watched a moment longer, than was swept up in a torrent of rage when she noticed a familiar shoulder bag strapped across the old man's stoop.

A white plastic bucket filled with tools sat unattended at the curbside near where the men were working. A small hand pickaxe was clustered in with other tools. She walked over and removed the axe. It was unexpectedly light and rested comfortably in her hand.

The thick metal arc that crossed the top of the foot long wooden handle was rusted and scared. She wondered why she hadn't sought out the comfort of such an instrument sooner. A few people saw what she had taken and walked on with a heightened sense of urgency.

The old man shuffled along as Kelly recalled, to her delight, a time when she could scamper down a block with her sister in a breath, turn around, and tag up where she began, faster than any child in the neighborhood. Now, more than twenty years later, that same fire and force of youth and focus was rekindled in her damaged legs. By the time she heard the angry cry of the scavengers and their apparent chase, she was halfway towards her target.

The pickaxe swung easily at her side. It was

reassuring. Comforting. And while there was injustice there had to be justice, and principles that would be the foundation of a rebirth of civilization. Kelly felt that truth, and a glow of optimism pulsed through her veins.

By the time she was a dozen yards away, people were standing back against the stores and moving into the street to avoid her and the gang in pursuit. The pain in her legs was as bad as it had been since the crash, yet hardly noticeable.

When there was no possibility of altering her path, the old man turned. His face was calm just as she had seen it in the antique shop. His warm green eyes revealed neither fear nor surprise.

"You're making a very foolish mistake," she expected him to say as the rusted tip of the pickaxe swung downward moments before a flash of green burst from a patrol ship high overhead.

As the point of the pickaxe plunged through a mat of wispy white hair, the old man's face changed into that of the young man to which she had first been attracted. Then, as the metal point speared through flesh, another face appeared. A woman in her late fifties with oily skin and a genetically unfriendly grimace. Once the resistance of cranial bone was breeched another face, and then another, morphed, until half a dozen faces appeared and withered before the green flashed warmed, then incinerated Kelly Christina Ramos' bones and viscera in an incandescent puff.

In one withering explosion, a sigh of relief raced through her tortured soul. She only wished she could have been a spectator at her own death and witnessed her joyous rebirth, and conjured the image of a plume of doves as they gushed out of her heart and into the promise of a better tomorrow.

The Unwelcome Guest

Hatch watched the lone fly coming straight for him. It stopped its diving assault just short of the tip of his fishing pole and hovered watchfully.

"I will skewer you. I will cut you to ribbons you fool. I will make you dance for your dinner. Plead for your life. Beg for mercy. But there will be none. Not today. Not ever," he said in his best mocking French accent as he brandished the flimsy bamboo pole like a dueling foil at the fly. The fly withdrew to a safer distance as the pole and the fishing line flailed about. Donald Hatch did not speak a word of French but felt impersonating the language lent authenticity to his display of contempt.

The pole nearly slipped out of Hatch's left hand as he repeated his threat and began to laugh. But he managed to wrap his fingers back around the narrow cork grip without losing the bottle of beer in his right hand.

"There," he said proudly as the fly approached the tip of the steadying pole. "You taunt me. Challenge me. Ridicule me," he said, slurring the derisive word until it bore no resemblance to the tone of its original construct. "Just keep away from me."

As the pole steadied, the fly began a slow, purposeful decent along the shaft from the tip. Wafting left and right, over and under the pole, as though still unsure of its safety, until it finally alighted on the chrome fishing reel.

"Smartass little shit," he said flicking it away with his index finger. But the fly anticipated his inept counterattack, feigned right and looped back on the reel like a seasoned prizefighter dodging a badly telegraphed blow.

Hatch shot out his hand and grabbed for the fly but it simply darted higher, out of reach. He leaned forward and it dropped off to his left. He went to snatch it out of the air and each time it evaded his tired grasp. He was surprised at his adversary's dexterity. Another fly passed close to his head but flew back out to the center of the lake that swarmed with them at this time of the morning. This one was more obvious about its intentions.

It was early, possibly not more than seven-thirty, and already the August day was warm and thick with moisture. By noon it would be impossible to breathe. By then he would be at work teaching ungrateful, pimply morons to spell and identify verbs from adjectives. Maybe, if he could get himself off the dock without falling into the lake, find the keys to his truck, and drive the eight miles to Larrimore Junior High School without speeding by the security gate. And, if he could park his truck without sideswiping another.

He lifted his second beer to his lips and took the balance of the bottle in a long series of sweet gulps. He could hear it drop down his gullet. Feel it fire his gut.

"Either you had one, or you were a pansy,"

Jennings, his old drinking buddy from Altoona, Pennsylvania, bragged. "A gut says you are not afraid to step up and take a gulp from the juices of life."

Hatch didn't have a gut. His metabolism kept him rail thin even at thirty-eight, no matter what he ate or how much he drank. But there were other ways he could prove himself a man. He pulled the neck of the third bottle across a wood plank underfoot until it caught the edge, hooking on the bottle cap and ripping it from the top of the bottle. He finished off the third bottle without taking his eye off the fly that continued to dance brazenly around the reel.

"You got a gut, asshole, or are you one of them candy-assed pansy flies?" he asked, ending the question in booming laughter.

Hatch thought the fly pulled back as his laugh gradually increased in volume. He tried laughing again, falsely this time, to see if it had the same effect, but he must have been wrong. It was the beer. If he drank too early in the morning, which he often did of late, then the effect was more profound. His body parts began to function on their own, with an alarming, uncontrollable independence.

The fly buzzed around his right hand then, quite unexpectedly, as if it had designed its day with this one foolish stunt in mind, shot at Hatch's chest, and slipped between the buttons in the crack in his shirt. Hatch dropped the pole and frantically reached in and searched with his hand until most of the buttons were torn from his shirt. He jumped around on the dock as if he'd been attacked by a swarm of killer bees, then pulled his shirt from his pants and ripped off his t-shirt.

"Come on. Come on," he repeated as if he couldn't say it fast enough. In his haste, he had kicked over the two remaining bottles of his six-pack, barely saving one as the other rolled from the pier into the lake. He propped it up against one of the vertical posts supporting the pier. He was sweating. Out of breath. He couldn't remember what he was doing before he kicked the beer overboard.

This wasn't like the incident last year with the ants over in Bridgeham High School. That was, as Doc Winters put it, a result of too many drinks over too many years. But Hatch was never positive that he wasn't really attacked by the fire ants. He scratched and scratched for days. Broke into waves of cold sweat and uncontrollable shaking. Every inch of his body was covered in ulcerating welts as he fought them off. In exhaustion, he relented and accepted his temporary madness for what it was. Questionable.

But this was different. Yet there was no fly. Maybe it was caught in his crumpled shirt. Or maybe it got away when he was searching for it.

And then he noticed a sinister speck sticking to the skin about eight inches to the right of his navel. One moment it was there, the next it was gone. It had burrowed into his flesh. He watched, fascinated and confused. But he wasn't hysterically frantic anymore. A drop of blood slipped from the wound but there was no discomfort. Then the fly was gone. Disappeared. Hatch looked around but he was alone, half-naked, with a tiny red hole in his right side, his shirt and t-shirt coiled around his feet. He became nauseous and fell dizzy to the dock, making sure not to lose the last bottle of beer.

He picked it up, yanked back the cap and took a deep, reassuring gulp. He was never going to make class by nine o'clock. He was going to be fired. It was the third time this month he wasn't there to substitute for absent summer school teachers. He would have to move again. Falsify documents and his teaching credentials. No one ever checked them anyway. All they wanted was a body to serve their needs. Just like the fly.

He touched the wound. Another drop of blood dripped. He picked at it. Then he pushed his index finger into the wound. It sank into his side. He was startled. Dumbstruck with surprise. He pulled out his finger. It was slicked red. He wiggled it as if he had discovered a remarkable, new instrument. He plunged it into the hole and pulled it out. He repeated the process several times until he was certain of himself. The hole in his side had stretched to the width of his index finger.

Fortunately, depending on your point of view, Hatch's fingers were quite thick. His wrists were thick as were his hands. Whenever anybody commented on his fingers or wrists and a woman was about, he would say, "That's not all about me that's thick." Only his thumb was heavier. As thick as the handle of a hammer, his first wife said once. He thought it was a reason for pride. Later he found out that she only spoke about her husband to others in one tone. Derisively.

He looked around again. As if some of his friends were lurking in the bushes prepared to proclaim him the butt of a practical joke. But he was alone. He pressed his fingers around the rib cage on his right side. It didn't hurt. He inserted his index finger up to the base knuckle and probed about. He could feel his ribcage, one rib, then another. He hooked his finger and thought he could make out the wall of his stomach. He was fascinated by what he was doing, then remembered what had turned him to such grotesque behavior. The fly was in there. Inside his body.

He had gone through the eleventh grade and passed a general studies course in biology. He didn't care for insects, but wasn't ignorant of their behavior. He knew that all they did was breed and what they used as the source of their sustenance. He knew what was going on inside in body. His skin crawled with the certainty that he was being taken over. Used, as a host, to an eventual and consuming infestation.

Hatch started to turn. He would race back to his car and go into town and get Doc Winters to examine him. Then what? What if Winters, who was too old to practice five years ago, couldn't find anything? Or what if he simply didn't believe him? He had also been to Winters three years ago spouting stories about having seen UFO's on Carter's Ridge. But that was because he was already crazy drunk. That was different.

He held onto the vertical support, dipped his hand into the lake, and washed the smeared blood from his side. He felt better when the wound was cleaned. When he realized he had a bottle of beer left, he fell to his knees and finished it off. He jammed his finger into the mouth of the bottle and flipped it up into the air. Before it splashed into the lake, he pushed his finger into his side as deep as it would go.

But there was no fly. No small, unwanted object curled up in a recessed corner of his innards. There was nothing except his frustration and the beat of his heart. His finger was poised at the top of his stomach. He thought he could feel something tear between the lungs and stomach but, since he felt no pain, he couldn't be positive he'd injured himself. He wanted to avoid that if possible.

That's what was so unusual about all this. Hatch felt nothing. Not the gash in his side, not his poking about, not pushing in on his internal organs, though he wasn't quite certain which gooey gelatinous mass was which. He pushed harder, trying to get better access when the gash in his right side split open. He quickly pulled out his finger. His entire hand, not simply the index finger and his knuckles, were reddened. The wound was now big enough to accommodate two or three fingers. His entire fist if he was so inclined.

He looked about again. No beer left. He was on his own. No job to return to. No life worth mentioning. This had to be a dream. A nightmare. But it wasn't. Bubbles on the surface of the pond where fish were coming up for air, the raven's cry out in the thicket to his right, the swarm of flies hovering in the center of the pond. He knew about the swarms of midge flies that billowed up with each full moon on Lake Victoria in Africa. He knew how their brown mass consumed miles of sky and dominated life for hundreds of miles in every direction. He knew how they terrorized all who stood in their path.

What if they attacked? No time for that now, only the urgency at hand. He leaned to his right so his head dropped as close to his ribcage as possible and pulled back a flap of skin. Instead of stretching, it came away, opening up a large hole, as if he had pulled back a sheet of wallpaper. Instead of plasterboard, there were ribs and muscle and fiber. And movement. Like he had peeked into the Big Tent of the world's most unusual circus. He pulled a little more and the flap widened, revealing the pulsating base of his heart. He was staring at his essence. He was watching his heart pump him alive. Hatch was watching his own goddamn heart.

"This is amazing. Fucking, unbelievably amazing," he said.

The right side of his body from hip to shoes was covered in small red droplets, but neither the loss of blood nor the gaping wound through which he could easily pass a softball, had any effect on his stability or coherence.

"I gotta show this shit to somebody," he said spinning around, as if an audience was waiting for his presentation. "No, not yet," he said catching himself.

There was the problem of the missing fly, which by now had staked out a piece of Hatch's viscera for himself. Who was at this moment multiplying, duplicating, furthering its species at the expense of Donald Hatch, substitute teacher to the masses. What he had to do could only be completed in private, and never recounted to anybody lest he be called a madman.

"Madman," he murmured quietly.

Doc Winters would throw him out of his office if he came by with this tale. He'd take one look at the gaping wound, stitch him up entombing the fly, and have him committed for observation.

Hatch needed a drink. Badly. Quickly. No store was going to sell him a six-pack at this hour, and certainly not with this minor problem. He had to get the fly, get covered up, and get a drink. Quickly.

Hatch jammed his hand into his guts and probed around with a renewed sense of urgency. He ran his fingers along his small intestines then the large intestines. He was amused and amazed at how clearly and simply the excavation went. No pain or spasms of apprehension, or gush of blood. He was focused, taken with a sense of absolute clarity. His mission was too important to be diverted by a faint heart, even if he could actually see it.

The more Hatch probed, the faster his heart pumped. The faster it pumped, the more captivated he became with its throbbing pulse and the more it reacted to the visual input of its own existence. Hatch knew no man had ever experienced what he was witnessing. No doctor had ever had a live cadaver on which to experiment, to test and prod and manipulate. He sat on the top of one of the vertical piles supporting the pier, glaring into the heart of Hatch's heart.

"No man has come before me and none shall come after," he said trying to recall the biblical reference, than he realized he had heard it in a soap opera. He laughed. His insides jiggled. He laughed again. His insides convulsed. He flicked his rib. One, then another, like he was playing a xylophone. He took a deep breath and his lungs expanded. He exhaled and the gleaming gray balloons contracted.

But there was no fly. He continued to poke about but couldn't find the fly. Finally, he realized that he would have to go deeper. If he was to rid himself of this pestilential threat than he would have to make a greater commitment. There was no point in looking around for help. He was alone except for the ravens, fish, and the pocket of flies that hovered over the space where he had first cast his line. Where he thought the fly that had gotten into his body had come from.

They were watching him. Hatch could tell. They were watching and calculating and laughing at him. They were making odds and taking bets that he wouldn't find their brother, and laughing at him. He could hear the swarm laughing. It gave him reason to pause.

Hatch watched them hover right over that spot

on the lake. He'd been coming down here since he was a kid. Always, the same spot and always the same success. He knew every cove and contour of this lake. It had been good to him and for its generosity, he had kept it a secret. From friends in school to friends who stayed with him through two wives, too many jobs to mention, six months in jail for assault, and a stay in the county hospital after he rammed his motorcycle into a brick wall after a night of drinking.

Hatch sensed this was a defining moment in his life. He'd had several already and knew they demanded complete attention and resolve. There was the time he found out his second wife was cheating on him. The time he found out his parents never loved each other. The time he knew he didn't have the intellectual capacity or curiosity to become the architect he had wanted to be from childhood. And soon after that, the times he realized he didn't care if he got fired, or about the value of what others thought of him.

This was such a moment. This was a clever, insidious adversary who had sacrificed itself and was prepared to take Hatch with him. Hatch examined his wound. It was no longer a point of curiosity or amazement. It was Hatch. Or part of the man that he never thought he would be privy to. There was no one to help him through this but himself. There was a rumble in his center, coming from his stomach. He stopped moving so he could listen. It was churning up from his stomach. A loud belch rumbled up from his belly until it came out in one sickening cacophony that brought a grimace of relief to his face.

"Sounds good to me," he said, first noticing the swarm of flies had drifted from their spot in the center of the lake. The faint gray cloud was now smaller, darker, more concentrated. They had tightened their formation.

Hatch wanted a drink. He needed one badly. Now. Not in a while, or later, or at some distant date he might never reach. Those fire ants were real. Doc Winters was an incompetent fool. He should never have trusted him. The two blue UFO's and the smaller red one were real too. These were defining moments no one believed in. No one understood. Hatch's lips smacked together. He recognized the habit. Right before he began to shake, he began to get a tightening feeling around his lips. On a woman it might be described as a pucker. On this man it was a warning.

At first he thought the formation was becoming still denser. Then Hatch realized it was moving in his direction. It was getting smaller, more focused. Closer. He moved back a few steps almost stumbling over his fishing pole, the lightning rod for his current predicament. He imagined flies converging from every part of the lake into this cloud that grew still darker and larger all at once.

"What do you want?" he yelled out. The index finger on his left hand, dripping red, pointing accusingly in their direction.

He pulled up his pants that had drooped so low they were making it impossible for him to move about. He could run for cover, but only his car assured him of complete safety. That was up on the crest of the hill overlooking the lake. If he was going to make a run for it, he had better do it now.

Then he realized what was happening. It was a diversion. How clever. How diabolically cunning they were. There was a plan here. They were distracted him so that he could not attend to what was eating away at his insides.

"Not this time, you bastards."

He could see his car. Maybe thirty yards, but it was all uphill. He glanced over his shoulder. He had to get enough momentum while he was on the flat pier to carry him up the hill. So much to think about, to devise, and follow through without a drink. Without a drink, even the slightest nuance of life was a giant hill he had to climb with no legs, he'd once told a counselor. The social worker nodded unsympathetically and gave him another appointment for the following week. Hatch tore up the slip of paper and never returned to the State clinic.

He was running hard. He didn't want to look down to see what was happening to his insides. He imagined that if he ran too long they would spill out of the opening. He was almost to the shoreline at the end of the pier. He would get to his car and drive to town and find a beer and pour it right into the wound and drown the fly. How ingenious, he thought just before he slammed into one of the support poles. He staggered back, clutching his side. He began to cough uncontrollably. His chest exploded in racking, convulsive pain. He noticed a group of women walking along the shoreline but they were so far away he couldn't be certain if he knew any of them.

In trying to regain his balance, he tripped over his own feet and fell from the pier into the lake. He gulped in water. He could feel the cold flood his insides. Filling him up. His body quickly sank to the bottom.

It was drowning the fly. That was something he had never thought of doing. He reached down and grabbed onto a rock until he was secure. Until he was certain the fly would drown if only he could hold on.

Donald Hatch, of 21 Suffern Street, was pulled

from the bottom of the lake not ten minutes after the three women notified the police. But it was too late.

There was nothing unusual about the drowning or the physical condition of the victim. The fact that he was so intoxicated would have explained why he drowned in only five feet of water, but not why the paramedics had to pry one of his hands lose from a rock, and a fly out of the other.

Dionaea Muscipula

If you walked down a street and found a man covered in a black shroud, would you assume that pacing off another block would reveal another of God's fallen angels? I didn't know the answer so I decided to walk the extra block.

I was undecided what I would do if I came upon a similar object. Knowing that since I had not fully examined the first body there was no assurance that the second wouldn't simply be a duplicate of that soul. I would therefore be disposed to believe that the second was merely a mystical reflection my mind projected of the first and thankfully not another strewn in my path.

When I turned the corner, I saw a second figure cramped into the same position, again with a filmy, transparent black shroud covering every inch of the body except for the feet. How then, you might ask, did I know what was under the first or second shroud if I failed to uncover the first and hadn't yet reached the second? I was seriously dismayed by the quandary set before me.

Of course, I did walk close enough to the first to make out the vaguest profile of the stricken soul. I would judge he was a man in his early forties. A hiker like me, his backpack was so fused to his body he looked like a sleeping hunchback. I couldn't make out much more from the hesitant position I took up near the curb. I half expected him to throw back the shroud, smile at me, and confess this had all been an elaborate plot to catch me off guard or even better, a ruse to be the first to wish me a happy seventy-fourth birthday, which was only a week away. But, as I feared, there was no life left in the man.

A cool blue wind swept up one street, made a hard left turn, and blew down the next. I was engulfed by the sweet-smelling vapor. I inhaled and smiled. It smelled like strawberry cotton candy on a hot August day. As a child, I would beg my parents to take me to the traveling carnivals that squatted in the open fields that surrounded my hometown. I loved the clanking Ferris wheels, the frolicking carousel horses, the temptation of the brass ring, and the pink cotton candy that my mother peeled from my exuberant cheeks at the end of the summer day.

The transparent shrouds that covered both bodies fluttered up for the briefest moment by the spiral breeze revealing what lay underneath. Indeed, they were dead men in a state of consummate indifference. I believe that is how indifference should be so defined, by its state of consumateness. It's not enough to be detached from the world and those around you. You must take that remoteness and make it your own before you can reach the peace both these men had apparently achieved.

Now what would be the prudent thing to do at this crossroads? Which, if either, deserved my immediate attention? The answer to that was quite simple. I alone deserved my most immediate and ardent attention. Does it not make sense to attend to my own wounds before I could wrap and heal those of my fellow man? And what if one or both were already too far gone to benefit from my ministrations? What then of my wasted energy that would have been better spent curing my growing mental and physical decrepitude?

I stood marveling at the blue wind. The ocean blue, ethereal essence snaked and wove its way through the deserted streets of this peculiar, forbidden place. I had long been captivated by the color blue in all its earthly and heavenly majesty. I can't recall when I first noticed it caroming around the unkempt maze of two and three-story buildings. I licked the taste of the strawberry vapors from my lips. I could feel the rich succulence drain into my stomach. I had half of a bottle of fresh, cold spring water in my knapsack but was reluctant to dilute the fruity sensation even though I was quite thirsty. I glanced up toward the midday sun and searched the sky for the birds of Maine. There were none. But I knew they would return if I wished hard enough.

I opened my sweat-stained tunic. There was nothing within but a frayed cotton shirt that Delia had given me long ago. I didn't feel the need to search for what I sensed was ailing me, so I buttoned it up again and considered my options, limited as they appeared to be. Could either of these men contain a spare part, something I could cannibalize in order to bring my body into line with my senses?

Again, I was left with the same question. Whom to tend first? When I turned my back on one and focused my attention on the other, I was instantly overcome with doubt and guilt for having abandoned the first. When I reversed my position, the same combination of doubt and guilt overcame my equilibrium. I slumped to the ground, weary with indecision.

I felt a pounding in my skull. It was not like me to have headaches. Then again, it was equally unlike me to wander from my appointed path in an incapacitated fashion like some schoolchild who had been blown off course by the billowing sails of his imagination.

Then the puzzle twisted once again in the wind. What if, for arguments sake, such a stranger should appear and firstly, I might not be able to get his attention, or secondly, he might not want to attend to my needs even if I did get his attention, or thirdly, that if he did come to my rescue he would be able to offer any solutions which I had not previously considered? Then again, he could be a she. Feeling overcome with a sense of dissolution, I could no longer work through any more of the conundrum. I felt myself growing weaker, spiraling downwards, a corkscrew of deepening despair into a shallow, faded darkness.

I do not know how long I slept or what I dreamed or if I dreamt at all. The sun had moved little in the sky. The wind blew, dusty and dirty as before, and I did feel somewhat renewed. Each of my two companions remained in place.

It was important to remain calm, alert, and reason myself through this quest. This was a town, like any other. I was a man of seasoned reason. I would resolve the mystery in my favor as I had done all my life.

That's when I heard the noise and saw the shooting star in the sky. It may not have been a true shooting star, but the round disc was shooting across the heavens when I first noticed it. It was quite large and, I believe, yellow. Then it stopped. Yes, I said it stopped and hovered directly overhead. I was as suspicious as you may be reading this account, but believe me, it was as much of a surprise to me as was coming upon the two disconsolate figures. The heavy laboring sound emanating from the ship reminded me of a diesel engine that was about to succumb to unnatural forces. It was no more than eight hundred, maybe a thousand, feet above me. Evidently, I was not the only one plagued by the quandary of these two bodies. But, try as I might, it was difficult for me to conceive that this irrational sight in the afternoon sky was the assistance I so dearly sought.

There was no way for me to communicate with either them, or them with me, even if they noticed my stooped, shadowy figure near one of the lesser buildings of this lesser town. There was little doubt in my mind that the two shrouded men were not visible from much greater distances.

Then the low thundering groan quickly changed pitch into a high whine and, as quickly as it appeared, the spacecraft sped away and disappeared into a dot over the horizon. I was alone again. And I was failing the test.

I moved from the curb back to the edge of the three story brick building at the corner of Mercer and Hudson streets. To my left were the boarded remains of Tyson's Liquor Store. To my right, the wreckage of Digby's Dry Goods Store. From the looks of their shattered interiors, both outlets would have been more at home in a history text of early nineteenth century Americana rather than associated with the context of present twenty-first century technology.

From this vantage point, I could see down Hudson and Mercer, the respective locations where both men had either struggled until they were finally brought down by their own system failures, or some resident evil. No sooner had I settled in then I noticed movement coming from within the entrance of the abandoned Trilon Theater, diagonally across Mercer Street, from the comfort of my corner post. At first, it was difficult to make out. I could tell there was a stirring though its nature eluded me. If the wind hadn't picked up, I would never have been able to see the swirling fluid outline of another black gossamer shroud.

The two shrouds covering the bodies as well as this one were no larger than a child's bed sheet and as transparent as gauze, moving as if they would respond to my excited breath from a block away. I knew that was impossible. Though in a town of increasing impossibilities, what would one more matter? And of course, there was the problem of who had come before me and was either courteous or compassionate enough to cover these terminal malingerers? That alone was reassuring. I would soon be joined by either a resident or wanderer, Hopefully either would be more energized than I was.

The sweet-smelling blue wind created small dust devils, kicking up dirt and debris along the gutters and against the boarded retail stores. The faint tinge of blue, apparently a common sight in these unpredictable times, highlighted the movement of the dust devils more than they would have been had circumstances been otherwise.

The shroud danced around the entranceway to the theater until it spun out and into the center of Mercer Street, near where I had seen the first body. Then, to my surprise, a fourth shroud was swept from the doorway of the dry cleaners further up the street.

In seconds, a fifth and sixth shroud peeled away from what remained of Bannerman's Grocery Store, which I passed upon entering town.

The shroud with the theatrical background was behaving in a distinctly different manner than these three latecomers. Whereas the three other shrouds not covering the bodies moved about their particular space, this one behaved in a totally independent fashion, moving to the left and right, up and down the street with abandon, but never really drifting too far from the entrance of the theater or, for that matter, from me.

There were no automobiles in this town. No horses or buggies. It seemed like I had come to a crossroads where the only means of transport were your own legs and inspiration. I can't say that I wasn't intrigued. And I certainly wasn't leaving, even if I could overcome my sudden exhaustion, before I had sound reason in hand.

There were now four shrouds flying and spinning about in the wind like hysterical marionettes. Some reached heights of fifteen or twenty feet before they fell back to the surface of the street. And, except for the one in front of me, the others continued to demonstrate a preference for their own particular space, not moving up or down the street but remaining in a small circumference where they first took flight. Both bodies remained intact, the edges of their shroud flipping up and down as the bulk remained firmly in place, giving greater outline to the fallen figures. I believe one was considerably larger than the other. This could mean many things, including the fact that one could have been in that failed decomposing state quite a bit longer than the other had been.

The town of Bennett Falls had been deserted

for many years. This was common knowledge. Years ago, the town and its small population survived from work supplied by one of Maine's larger lumber mills. But when the mountain stands of maple and spruce were fully harvested, the mill was forced to shut down. Now its rusting hulk poisoned the land. I have come through town before, but I can't recall when I have felt so dissipated, so disinterested in where I was going or where I had come from.

At one point in my languor, I thought the man's body on Mercer had moved, if only imperceptibly. It might have. I just couldn't be certain. A man with one eye always doubts what lies before him. A man with one eye sees half of what the rest of the world notices and often survives by not putting himself in circumstances where only a man with two eyes could survive.

Even now, some fifty-eight years later, I doubt much of what goes on around me. I doubt my own reason, my logic, and my conclusions. It is only with my fears that I am totally assured of my footing. But where I am and what is occurring around me this day is no falsehood. Of that, I am certain.

The edge of the building cut up the center of my back causing a numbing sensation in my fingertips. I wiggled my toes. They seemed fit enough. And anyway, I was actually enjoying myself. I know that sounds cruel, what with those bodies lying in the street, but this mystery and the telling of it had an appeal that called to me like the sirens to Odysseus.

What had caught my interest now was that the shrouds had suddenly stopped swirling about as quickly as they began. Only the wind had not let up. Three shrouds were laid out, some folded over themselves in black clumps, while the one from the

Trilon was laid out flat on the street. I waited for something else to happen but it didn't, at least not with the vaporous black shrouds. I was anticipating the return of the spacecraft, or some other apparition that would be equally entertaining, and completely doubtful.

I rubbed my hands together in order to ward off the tingling that had intensified in my fingers. After some vigorous hand wrenching, I was able to resuscitate the flow of blood into my fingertips. But it was clearly a task. I looked into the sun-bleached sky, stretched out my legs and felt my body relax still further. Then, at the far end of Mercer, one of the shrouds spun up in a vortex of agitation. When it reached the height of the two-story building from which it sprang, it simply floated there for a second before descending back down to earth like a dying black dove.

I toyed with the idea of giving each of the six shrouds names. I thought of Snow White and the Seven Dwarfs, but I was one shroud short. I was fully prepared to make up the deficit by taking on one of the names. Grumpy would certainly be more descriptive of my natural personality although Sleepy was more befitting my current state. Maybe one more shroud was lurking somewhere else in town. Maybe there were more, hundreds more, about to make a more predatory entrance when they were convinced I was no longer in a position to fight or flee. Maybe the four unattached shrouds, and especially the one that bled from the Trilon and had what now appeared to be capable of more independent movement, had been sent out on patrol to reconnoiter my intentions and weakness.

I decided that the shrouds held my answers.

They were the key to solving the mystery of the two bodies that lay before me. However, while I was now more curious than ever, I felt uncharacteristically overcome with what could only be called an advanced state of lethargy, greater in its profound control over me than anything I had experienced before. A man of my age has already come in close contact with a range of alarming stimuli and harmful toxins in his life. Most have been warned off with moderate success. However, I was completely overtaken with the deepening stagnation that pervaded my body. I was relaxed. That was true. But I believed that was because I was near the end of my long hike, even if I was now uncertain of my exact location.

I mentioned the town of Bennett Falls to you. Well, I might have been a bit precipitous in my conclusion. Taking stock of the local merchants up and down Mercer and Hudson, abandoned and in disrepair as they were, it was now obvious that while all had colorfully descriptive names, none mentioned the town in which they were located. I was now positive that the turn I had taken on the trail an hour back must have been wrong. This was definitely not Bennett Falls. As a matter of fact, I had no idea where the hell I was.

What I was certain of was a sudden, sharp, piercing sensation in my lower back. I lurched forward. The pain subsided as quickly as it appeared, followed by a sensation of warm fluid flushing into my body. My lower back began to tingle in much the same way as my fingers did a moment ago. I couldn't fathom the feeling. I turned sharply to my left and right to see if someone was poking me. I was that unsettled by the memory of the sensation in my back. The activity or lack of it on Mercer and Hudson had not changed.

The streets hosted bodies, shrouds, and little else in the way of answers.

Delia would have known what to do. She always did. It's been almost two years since I lost her. We had forty-eight wonderful years together. She was the one who first got me interested in hiking and camping. Said I should take a pill to deal with my hay fever and get my sagging old ass out into the foothills of Maine. I miss her terribly. I always will.

My handicap, as I had always referred to my injured eye, was not a deterrent to Delia and her love for me. She never once looked at my black patch nor was swayed by my early disregard for prudence or my belief that, sooner or later, she would turn from me to a man with more balanced faculties. It was when she told me that her love was able to overcome my fear that I realized how fortunate I was to have her at my side.

She would have massaged the pain out of my back. She would also have told me that sitting against the edge of the building was something only a damn fool would do. I loved it when she spoke to me like that. The scolding, hovering, doting mother. So why was I sitting here immobilized as if my spine had been infused with the brick and mortar that was supporting it?

That's when I saw her. I was so shocked I actually rubbed my eye, thinking I had lost the balance of my mind. I waved but she didn't see me. I tried to get to my feet but something was holding me to the side of the building. I must have pinched a nerve. Things like that happen all the time when your bones get old and frail and your mind tends to wonder and lose track of the whereabouts of your extremities.

But I wasn't crazy. I wasn't going nuts. I was

watching Delia stroll down Mercer Street. She moved with the eager stride of a woman coming to meet her long lost lover. She was wearing her favorite, really my favorite, blue dress and short yellow jacket that ended just over her wonderful hips. I liked the way she moved in that dress and jacket. She still cut a smart figure. Then she noticed me. I felt both sickly and strange. It was bad enough I was hallucinating. I didn't need her appearance to confirm my weakening mental state.

The wind that had softened in these last few minutes began to stir again with the coming of Delia. The shrouds fluttered and flipped again, though with the constancy of the wind one would have thought that they would have been swept clear down the street by now instead of maintaining their original position. What matter? Delia was here. She would help me up. She would guide me from this maddening place.

"Hi, honey."

I was so startled to hear her speak to me I couldn't answer. Again, I tried to pull myself away from the building. The more I strained, the less my body answered. It was as if I had broken something inside that cut off sensation and motor control. What seemed broken was me.

"Did you see it?" she asked, standing in front of the theater on the other side of the street.

"What?" I answered, half suspecting she would disappear as soon as I spoke.

"The flying saucer. It was here a few minutes ago."

"The yellow flash in the sky?"

"Yes. Then you did see it."

My God. She was real. Delia wasn't dead. "Yes."

"I knew you would. That proves you're right.

That proves your theory about the existence of flying saucers. And I guess that makes me wrong."

I didn't want Delia to be wrong. I wanted her to run across the street, come to my side, and embrace me. I wanted to bound to my feet like I did as a younger man and take her in my arms and spin her about. Then, when she could no longer stand my uncontrollable enthusiasm, I would hold her so close to me that after a while our breathing would become as one.

"Come here," I said.

"No, you come to me. That's the way it has to be, my cute boy next door."

She would call me that in moments of deepest affection. We had been distant neighbors growing up in a small town outside Kansas City, Missouri. We had the same address number, just on different streets. I met her at a cotillion right after the Second World War, the one from which I was excluded because of my inadequate sight. I thought she was the most beautiful girl in the world. I believe she still is.

I strained to get to my feet and again the more I pulled against myself the more I could feel a warm flush spread throughout my body weakening me further. It was as if the building itself had taken possession of my body and would not release me from its invisible grasp. But I couldn't let her down. I couldn't leave Delia standing there. With what was left of my energy, I heaved myself to my feet. I had to, just this once.

I was not ill. I was in good spirits and feeling quite buoyant when I began my hike this morning. Indeed, I thought it would last only three hours and here it is, according to my wristwatch, already four hours have passed and I am still at a loss as to where

I am or why I am so thoroughly dissipated.

Before I could reach the curb, the black shroud that resided in the bowels of the theater rose as if kicked up by a sudden gust of wind. The wind that flooded Mercer and Hudson since my arrival and actually increased when Delia strode into town had now suddenly subsided. The blue essence that had so captivated me, had so taken my attention, had also vanished.

I stood the extent of my six-foot frame, proud and fulfilled. Delia came closer to the curb. "There's my boy. I knew you could do it."

With the contraction of one muscle, I could feel another collapse. I felt faint, and was just able to take the one step into the street. With that one movement, I briefly believed I could conquer all. Except that I was now convinced that something was wrong. Something was terribly, dreadfully wrong. The sharp pain in my back, which originally felt like a pinched nerve, now felt as if I had actually been stabbed. It was as though I was still carrying around the blade of my aggressor in my back. Whether it was a steel shaft or something used to deliver poison to my system was of no consequence to me. The effect was identical.

"There, now I'll come to you," my Delia said.

Her angelic face was as I recalled it on our tenth anniversary. She held out her hands to me. Just as I held out mine, I noticed the black shroud from the Trilon tossing and twisting in the still air some dozen paces to my right. I thought it miraculous and entertaining. I thought my circumstances mortally threatening. It was the only one of the six shrouds that had moved from the place of its origin and it was coming directly towards me.

Fearful of losing my balance, I forced myself

to turn my head as far as I could and glanced back towards the edge of brick wall where Mercer came together with Hudson. I expected to see a flat, plain brick facade. Instead, the wall had come alive. Its sides heaved with undulating bulges that ran up and down under the surface of the brick in a throbbing, pulsating rhythm that one could only associate with a heartbeat.

The facade that had once been rust-colored and streaked with mortar filling was now a glistening wall of dark green flesh mottled with streaks of faint yellow and black. A pair of short green tentacles with sharp, scalloped tips protruded from the point near the base of the wall about where I was resting. Two longer, massive tentacles were growing from the surface near the top of the two-story creature.

I held my contortion as long as I could, enabling me to witness the impossible. Both of the smaller, five or six-inch thin green tentacles began to withdraw into the roiling surface of the wall until all that remained of it was the most minute hole which I apparently did not notice when I chose the spot from which to observe my then unthinkable surroundings.

When I regained my posture, Delia was gone. Had she ever been here? Had she just been another shiny lure that caught me off guard long enough to be ensnared by this most elegant and poisonous trap? The pain in my back and legs became so excruciating I knew I would not be able to remain standing any longer. I would have called out for help but who would have heard my cry? High overhead the black shroud dancing in the still, clear, unsweetened air moved closer and closer to my untenable position.

The two bodies under their shrouds now made sense. But clarification to a dying man is worth considerably less than one might suspect. Insight learned too late is only useful to the next generation. They were dead. Of that, there can now be no doubt. That one had fallen before the other is no longer an issue. Soon both, as well as myself, will be absorbed into the beast that is this town, which, through its cunning and trickery, had enticed us to this closing state.

I collapsed to my knees as the black shroud continued its elegant pirouette high overhead. I noticed that it was larger than the other three. In fact it was not only larger than the three that accompanied it into the street, it was larger than the two that were clad over the dead bodies. And all six, I am afraid to admit now, had terribly irregular edges. I hadn't noticed this at first although I doubted it would have deterred me from this adventure. But it might have made a difference. At least I would like to think it would have given me pause to reflect and possibly retrace a path to safety.

I thought I smelled an acrid odor. But I couldn't be sure. Not of anything. I thought of warning off others who might come this way though I was in no position to save myself much less others so unfortunate. They might be smarter than I had been. Maybe not. Curiosity had a powerful calling, especially to one closer to the end of their life than the beginning. A challenge of your intellect against your senses, I suppose.

How many of us would have been strong enough to turn their backs on such a puzzle and save themselves from this terrible end? The three of us are testament to the compromising evil of our egos. We cannot have all the answers. Then again, what made me take that first wrong turn in the road before I was compromised by the poisonous blue wind?

I settled back on my elbows as the shroud lowered itself around me. Now, upon closer inspection, I could see that the black fabric was made of no common material at all but of small, insect-like creatures. As the acrid smelling shroud, like a giant jellyfish made up of thousands and thousands of infinitesimal organisms, fell over me, I could feel the poison that had been injected in my back by one of the green serpentine tentacles consume the remaining functioning nerve cells in my body. I fell numb onto my back, my eye flickering in uncontrollable spasm.

The shroud completed its engulfing descent. I took a few more pointless breaths and thought about how clever these creatures were to have persuaded my Delia to join in their deception. How clever indeed.

I Have Become the Leopard

Flies. Everywhere flies, biting, taunting, and sucking. A haunting, whispering cloud following me into sleep, pursuing every living creature long after they've died. They are part of the landscape as are the grassy plains, the wild brushfires, as the lion and rhinoceros, only far less particular about where they graze.

Overhead, a female hawk eagle searches for a meal that will sustain her children until they're strong and sufficiently trained to leave the nest. Under the fire of a searing African sun, she will cruise between the valley below and the vultures riding the crest of the warm currents above. Also searching. This is a nomadic life of combing and replenishing, as it has always been. I roll over onto my stomach, split my jaw open, and stretch out my forepaws. It's time to rise from the night and shake off the moisture from my coat. To beat a trail, though today I will not graze or forage unless game is readily available.

I rest back on my haunches, licking away the fire where the lion's claw ripped into my right hindquarter. Flies again, hunting for their morning meal, find my wound more than they had hoped. I chase them away with my tongue. It is soothing and will cleanse. If it doesn't heal, I will die. Not quickly, but all too soon.

Had I known the lioness was stalking the young Thomson's gazelle, I would not have pursued. I had come upon a fattened, spur-winged goose only the day before and was not grasped with hunger. But my instincts would not permit me to bypass such a satisfying opportunity. Having wandered off from the herd, the gazelle was grazing indifferently, as if it had abandoned reason and caution. Possibly, in the turmoil of a chase, as if it had separated from its mother. Or she had been taken by the pack of spotted hyenas I saw canvassing the perimeter of the herd. I crept to the fringe of tall grass and waited, vigilant that the wind might still turn against me. I thought the child was alone. I was wrong. Almost fatally so.

I was close enough, and fortunately not so aggressive as to launch myself sooner or I would have run headlong into the lioness who leapt from the bushes just as I did. We converged before either of us knew of the other's presence. The lioness swung around, sweeping out defensively with her forepaw as I spun and clawed myself to a halt. I've been wounded worse. Once, as a goshawk in an arid land, I lost a vital flight feather when a peregrine falcon shot from the sky in a withering attack. As a crocodile, I ambushed a herd of zebra crossing a swollen river, and for my resolve was savagely kicked, leaving the right side of my skull reeling in pain.

That I have been more successful than injured had lead me to my present path. I have killed so much game there is a blur of squealing and twisting, of feathers and crying froth. Pulsing squirts of blood crisscrossed my face and shot over my back as I disemboweled my prey. This day, and the next few, will decide if this life will end before I would have liked.

I have been many animals before. Flying, swimming, slithering, tunneling, prowling, but never have I been the leopard.

I move off from the swarms of flies that are drawn to my wound and lethargy. The sun crested in the sky long ago. But there will be no relief from the heat and the choking dust sucked up by the swirling winds; not until nightfall when the herds have eaten and satisfied themselves that they are safely through another day. By then I would have ranged at the heels of gazelles, gemsboks, wildebeests, and impalas, waiting along with the lions and cheetahs and pack dogs until my turn, and then cut out the weakest, most infirmed. It does not matter if you live in the air or water or roam in the dark for food as I do; the weak, slow and inattentive live out their lives quicker than most. And the lion does not draw a distinction between the unlucky and those with questionable judgment.

I can survive many days without making a kill, though not as long without water. I picked up the scent of water last night but the racking wound forced me to discontinue my drive. I sought refuge, sanctuary. It is too early to judge the measure of my narrow escape. Though today the pain does not feel as threatening. I can still see the lioness's open jaws. Startled, her instinct was to flail out, defend herself and take down the intruder with one vicious swipe of her paw, indignant, annoyed that I had warned the gazelle, and almost deprived her of an easy meal. Had I not been as agile, had she not been, for just a second, indecisive as to whether she wanted to pursue the gazelle or punish the intruder, I might not be here—wound, hunger, thirst and all.

The wind shifts, a trio of suricates stand

lookout on top of their raised mounds searching the horizon for food and danger. These mongooses are too far away and, at the mouth of their burrow, unreachable. I have had them before, but not as a leopard. And this sensation of knowledge rings alone where before there was silence. I recall crushing the neck of the mongoose and watching its life spread red around my paws, but only because the taste of it is less desirable than most prey. A distinction I have never made before.

I also recall slashing the throat of a newborn impala, also not as the three-year-old leopard I am. These memories, events that do not come to mind naturally, are easily misplaced or overwhelmed by the immediacy of my journey on the plains. Yet, there is a difference. If I survive this wound, I might live long enough to understand. Though I do not know what advantage that will give me when evading those who pursue me, or locating those upon who I feed.

What I feel, the spirit of my past is different than before. The fact that I can recall a before, an image, events, escapes, and kills assuming other forms, is something I have not seen in the eyes of other animals. I have become aware of myself, that my life and circumstances and relevance that are being fed by a force I cannot clearly identify. Perhaps that is best. My struggle must be confined to the present, not distracted by speculation of my past.

Impala ahead. The pungent scent of their musk and droppings is strong on the wind. As it will be for all the great cats and those who plunder in pursuit and scavenge behind their tailings. This lesson I learned from my mother. Looking up, staring at the blood-soaked coil attached between her shaking legs to a place where I began. It is a vision I will never forget. And it was in that same instant I recalled the male gharial I was before this birth. And in moments of flight and recent reflection, a bonobo, the pygmy chimpanzee, dancing from limb to tree, delighting between the green canopy and gold sky which left me with a freedom I've seldom found.

Now I am of the earth. Leaving scent and stalking scent. Tethered to grass, scrub, and sand I must make do with the hearts of springbok, gazelle, and eland, and the ancestors of those I've been. I prefer the sweet, gentle taste of ming berries, the tight thickness of nuts found only high in the forest, the lingering softness of bananas and tang of mangos. Though springbok and gibbon seem preferable to fish and floating carrion.

She severed the link between us with her teeth and washed me with her tongue. We were one. For many days, we remained close, until I learned what she and my ancestors had taken a lifetime to collect, and now, because of a lion's flashing claw, it may not be enough. I recognized her smell before anything. Her touch was new, only her tongue was strange. I scampered to my feet, momentarily blind, but already alert to her stirring. She was vulnerable because I was at her side. And I, like all children, would be for some time. She brought me kill, sacrificing herself that I may be nourished and grow.

Her insides remained fresh to me until my maturity drove me from the pack, or was it her natural insistence? That day the sky blackened and roared, as would a wounded lion. Rain fell for days after. I sought protection in a granite outcropping that sheltered me from the torrent and my loss. Except for the light in my mother's eyes, I've never seen the sparkle of comprehension in others that I see in pools of watery reflection. The look in the eyes of macaws and giraffes are quite similar. Spirits driven from one dawn to the next dusk to spend the night in seclusion and not succumb by accident or fate to the jaws of a more adept predator. This difference troubles me. When left to my own, to wander, to hunt, to establish my own territory, or to find a mate, it is ever on my mind. Why do I question my succession?

Another leopard joined her. They sniffed after each other but the hesitation was perfunctory. It was her sister. She sniffed me, establishing a link that instantly endowed me to her brood. There were seven of us. Myself, my mother, her sister, and her three offspring. That is not unusual. Floating as a goshawk, I know that leopards give birth to two or three cubs. Then I noticed the difference. My aunt's twin girls are a season older than the male who is not a week older than I. More protection for us in the future, but a greater handicap now. Two adults torn between five children. Many mouths to feed and protect from lions and worse, more deadly, the spotted hyenas.

With its solid build, high sloping shoulders, coarse coat, large muzzle, and long teeth, it is the second largest meat eater in Africa. The tan and reddish coat blends in with the scrub and parched underbrush. The spotted hyena will take down a bull wildebeest, and in packs that can range from twelve with eighty in reserve, fear nothing. It is the most ruthless, aggressive pack animal alive. Hyenas will not be intimidated or chased away from a kill. So pervasive is their thirst. An even earlier lesson learned.

My mother prodded me to my feet again and again that day. I preferred to roll about, taunt my siblings, and dance close to my aunt's tolerant side.

She was more severe than my mother. Utterly without emotion. Her children respected and feared her. They stood away, patiently distant until she came to rest, unsure unless she gave them a signal to approach and suckle. I took my mother's milk without permission and stumbled about making whimpering sounds of satisfaction she knew might endanger our safety.

That first day of life passed easily. I fell asleep. The pride did too. A rich land will do this. Food was plentiful. It is told in the eyes of the hunters. As a falcon, I traveled among the currents during storm and famine and watched. I always ate. When it rained, I feasted. When there was drought I was nourished by an ample supply of fresh carrion. There is no dry season for those of the air. Thus is my preference driven not by interest but by a thirst for life. Who would not want to be offered such permanency? There is less danger in the air than anywhere else. Not in the grass, certainly not clinging to the muddy riverbanks.

Am I the only one who is aroused by this conscious distinction? The first year of life told me so. I watched my brothers and sisters, their disorganized scampering preparing them to hunt and track and stalk and cut out the weakest from the herd and to race to that spot where the frightened might be directed. To make the most of each attack as the expenditure in time and energy is too great to waste. Like most cats, except for the lion who will kill and eat once in every four or five hunts, I will eat only once in ten. I will take food from the cheetah and pack dogs while relinquishing my kills to the lion and hyena.

This day I am hidden, patient in the underbrush, the wave of grass rises up on both sides protecting me as it did the lions yesterday. A herd of gazelle. Many will give birth in the coming days. Many will die in the coming weeks as hunters pick off the young and feeble. Only those who are born to speed, agility, and good fortune will escape and pass quickly into adolescence. Life in the herd is dangerous, though in the anonymity of such numbers, not without its benefits.

I rest. My hindquarter begins to burn, a sensation that does not concern me as long as it is soon relieved. If it is still inflamed by tomorrow, I will not live long. I wait for the scent of cats and pack animals, and those who fear them both. I hear only the sweep of wind scratching the top of dry grass. There is safety here, but no prey and no water. Yet, something else. The wind has shifted. I get up and pace about, still secluded, though unusually pensive. As though I should be moving on. I do not feel threatened as much as curious. There is something distinct and distant in the air. I knew it from before. From long ago, though I am uncertain in which life I first encountered it.

I move slowly away from the underbrush, constantly aware of my injury and limitations. I am the hunter. Wary. Always ready. Now I must think differently. Wild pack dogs, even a pair of hyenas, might tree me and simply wait for others to join in the kill. I am not who I was yesterday. I cannot concern myself with the possibility I may never be again

The scent intensifies. I pause and crouch, my snout to the soil. My hesitation is great, but I must not let it cripple me. I crawl closer as flies, once settled in the grass, are roused and swarm into my eyes, nose, and ears. A few lengths every so often. There is the smell of death. Of great defeat and greater danger. A covey of white-backed vultures begins to gather overhead. That will bring the lions and with them will come the hyenas. I have not much time. I cannot suffer curiosity at the expense of my life, which is already in great jeopardy

I should not have taken this course. I am wounded, no match for an encounter. I am no match for my own curiosity and combativeness. I decide to pull away when the wind shifts again, as it does at this time of year, unpredictably, and recognize the experience of death. I turn back into the wind, crouch down, and step to the fringe of the clearing. A giant beast of an elephant lies bleeding from a gaping wound in the side of its skull. Three creatures move about on their hind legs cutting away its two giant white teeth. They make quick, high pitched, unsettling noises. They lift the teeth and set them into something I have never seen, which swallows them whole and roars away. I watch apprehensively, as they trail off into a dry riverbed. Soon they are out of sight, though the dust kicked up from their flight can be seen for miles casting a shadow over the land.

I am left in doubt. Who would want elephant teeth? They have no value, cannot be eaten, or stored for subsequent meals, are of no importance in hunting except for those who first possessed them. How could these creatures benefit from such a conquest? And at the sacrifice of such a magnificent animal. I have seen these creatures before, not necessarily here, under this sun and not, if memory serves, merely as hunters. I will make an effort to clarify my suspicions, and not for purposes of curiosity, but rather so that I may be assuaged that I have not repeated a lifetime in such skin.

I get up and examine the carcass. It is a female elephant. The largest animal I have ever seen. The meat is fresh and there is moisture in fresh meat. There is also death. The vultures drop lower. The lions, even members of different prides, may be drawn to a kill of this size. I decide to withdraw downwind. As I take cover in the grass, I see pack dogs moving in from behind, their low murmuring howl signaling their intentions. If I stay, I will be caught in the savagery that is close at hand. I am no match for anything but healing.

I track a wide arc back to the trail of the impalas. They will lead me to water. I must drink today, or tomorrow I may not have the energy to venture out. Without water, even what remains in a mouthful of fox, I am going to die. The wound is not as painful, but it may fester and become deadly. I am exhausted and the sun has not yet joined the horizon. The incident with the lion has made me cautious, something unaccustomed to my nature.

My aunt was the first to encounter the maturity of my true spirit when I marked a tree already stained with the urine of a large male lion. She tried to warn me but I wouldn't have any of it. My mother came up after I had urinated and dropped feces at the base of the tree. It was foolish and I was dragged away. We never went back to the hillock. I do not recall why I was so defiant, other than the fact that I believed my territory was wherever I pleased to be.

That was some time ago, and yet my memory reaches further back in time, beyond my life and into the lives of gharials, eagles, and cobras. Among these echoes is an even stronger sensory pattern that I could only speculate upon. There are images, similar to those of the gibbon, but larger, whose habits and speech eludes my recall, but who I am uneasy about.

I come to a band of acacia trees stretching out for some distance. They will allow me to flank the impalas in cover and observe their watering hole. I prefer fruit trees, which attract less attentive parrots, trumpeter hornbills, African green pigeons, and starlings. From my vantage point, the sweep of the grassy plains opens up into a vision of ill-tempered animals roaming from one dry lakebed to another. The lush foliage is all but gone. Either eaten or burned off. Mudflats wither and crack. Even the hardiest will suffer. Some will dig watering holes under dry streambeds, but the brief gurgle will not support many searching tongues. Others will drop off from the herd and cling to strips and patches of forest, unaware that the lion, the most territorial of all animals, rests in their afternoon shadow. I have hovered above sand dunes, watched great nesting colonies of heron, ibis, and stork blacken out the sky in search of elusive freshwater marshes.

The rest of the afternoon is expended with getting into position, resting, and coating the wound with my tongue. There is nothing else to do but wait. The herd is made up mostly of impalas, intermingled with zebras and wildebeests. This is quite common and brings the entire herd into jeopardy as the mass of life grows to cover the grassland. I can live off many kills and, while instinct taught me to accept insects and birds, I've always preferred a chase before a meal.

What I prefer comes as a surprise. I prefer the gentle flush of tidal estuary waves against a mangrove, the small animals that live in the lowland rain forest, the simplicity of taking down a dik-dik, palm thickets that are free of flies, the highlands and verdant plateaus, stalking flamingos in seasonally flooded marshes, the taste of palm nuts, warm and humid air and heavy rain, dense foliage, scrubby grassland whose only attraction is enormous baobab tress with branches sheltering nesting blue-bellied rollers, parrots, and barbets. Savannah woodlands with wide grassy plains, gallery forests, rivers flanked by borassus palms and thick with duikers, red-fronted gazelles, bushbucks, patas monkeys, scissor-tail kites and cranes. Always cranes, whose flesh I prize above all others.

A large troop of savannah baboons, the largest of its family, advances into the path of the impalas. There are about thirty of them, though troops can amass up to two hundred animals. There is nervousness among the herd. A new species attracts new predators. The mix is unsettling. However, the baboons, themselves capable fighters, expend their energy cleaning and preening and gathering into clearly defined groups. The dominant females and males, the children skittering among the elders, searching for approval and acceptance. They scream, mate, eat, and rest under the broad canopy of branches. It is in those branches I would have taken my next kill. Into those notches in the high branches, I would have carried my prey secure in my jaws. It is in those branches, safe from other cats, I would eat. However, not today. Now I am as earthbound as the rhino, though there the comparison ends.

Soon I am alerted. The wind has not shifted, though there is something close by. I do not fear the intruder but the impalas should. I lift my head and see the thick golden collar of a massive lion. He is shepherding two other males into position. They are there for the ambush, not for the kill. That will be left for the females waiting on the other side of the herd. A well-orchestrated technique will take down one or two large impalas and will amply feed the lion pride. If they get wind of me and feel I have compromised their hunt, I will be chased down and killed. I drop myself down to the earth as they pass close by.

The two male lions rouse the herd, which stampedes toward the waiting females. As the trap is sprung, I get to my feet. I am taken by their contained stride, by the effortless power of their assault, their graceful arrogance, and the presumption of their heritage. This is their land. Every other creature is here at their sufferance. They will not condone temerity or transgressors. I cannot help but wonder what it would be like to be a lion. To be totally fearless. To be totally feared.

Thoughts like these lead me to question my past, which does not augur toward a successful future. It is at best a point of interest animals do not possess. Then if that is true, what does that make me? Am I more than the leopard? The sum of my past?

The dust settles. Overheated lions decorated with bloodstained muzzles stand triumphant over two dead impala. There are eight lions with enough fresh carrion to keep the pride content. As soon as the herd sees that the kills are complete, they return with excessive energy to grazing and securing their young. Toward the fringe of the herd is a broad watering hole surrounded by clusters of uprooted junipers that have long succumbed to the elephant's destructive feeding habits. A family of zebra staked out one side of the watering hole, while baboons gather on the other. Impalas slip in between.

I must drink. The thirst is making breathing difficult. My heart races to keep my body cool. I could wait another day, but then I would be weaker, more vulnerable. Less audacious. Then there would be no room for any more miscalculations.

Under the mask of confidence, I move out of the clearing. At this heightened pace, my injury is deeply uncomfortable. Before the vultures signal hyena and lion, several impalas notice my presence. They whinny an alarm which sweeps through the herd. I pick up speed, not making for the watering hole at first, but in that general direction. They scatter, reminded of the more fearsome pride that attacked only moments earlier. The baboons pull back from the watering hole, not frightened, though heedfully suspicious. The zebras lift their heads indifferently. A zebra has nothing to fear from leopards. I approach the pool, stop, scan the horizon, growl contemptuously at a clot of frightened elands, and proceed to drink. More than necessary, but anxious that it may be my last.

The water is cold. I cannot wait too long as my weakness may alert others, especially the two young approaching hyenas. They glance over at the muddy waterhole, and then continue their advance on the lions. In the distance, double their number head toward the lions at a pace that will quickly bring them into confrontation. I take one last gulp and leave, aware that I must not let on how difficult this journey has been.

That night I sleep in the crown of a broad acacia. I have found an old tree with a thick branch that is over three of my lengths from the ground. I am fearful that being too close to the herd will draw my enemies to me. I need the herd, for if I am to live, I will have to make a kill soon. If they leave, I will follow. If not, I will remain here until I heal or die.

Tonight the memories return. A mass of steep canyons. Mountain ranges and the inland plateau edge of a great escarpment. Dry lakebeds. Remnant ponds. Mass migrations of grazing animals, flamingo, and stork. A maze of channels, papyrus swamps, wet swales, rocky outcroppings, towering green mountain ranges, and mountaintops covered with stunted woodland, standing over the kills of a golden jackal and a red fox. Is it that I am so close to death that my past, and the past of others I have been, wells up so easily? Finally, the image of an adult male impala presents itself. I do not recall details of that life. I am grateful for not recalling the details of that death.

Sometime during the night I am awakened, but not by danger. I open my eyes and look down. A female African hare moves about in search of nuts and insect burrows at the base of the tree. She is not aware of my presence. This would make a tidy meal but under these circumstances, unable to leap from this height without endangering my wound, she is safe. She fills her mouth and scurries on into the night. The moon gives away her position, as it would have mine had I not taken to the trees. An adult female topi grazes in her path. She turns to avoid it and disappears in the grass. The topi presented no threat. In darkness or light, there is never safety.

The ones who claimed the elephant reappear in my sleep, as though there was a singular kinship calling me to their side. From the sky I have watched their stirring, where they wander and how they hunt and the fact that they do not stalk or ambush, rather, simply interpose themselves in the tracks of an animal and the beast succumbs. I do not understand. If this is true, then we all are doomed. Such is the greatness of their hunting skills. There is no sanctuary in the rain forest, the forest or savannahs, in the lush rolling grasslands or stands of evergreen. Not in the air or in the water. I have seen them hunt bird and now the majestic elephant. How easy it is for them. How strange they never feast on their kill though their exultation was quite evident.

The next morning I am aroused, but it's not by a hungry plains hare. Two hyenas linger where the hare was foraging. They are onto her scent. I cannot stir for fear I will be detected. They will remain at the base of the acacia until their search is rewarded or they are attracted by other game. They lift their heads. They have caught another scent. Mine. Neither can make a location, but they persist. There is a commotion in the distance, in the direction where the lions made their kills. It distracts the hyenas. One draws the other out from under the canopy and together they trot off together toward the rising cloud of dust and opportunity.

A female cheetah stalks an impala. The herd is swelled with newborn. A nursing herd is a favorite killing ground, especially for the cheetah that, although it is the fastest animal on the plains, gives up much of its kill to more powerful hunters. The cheetah's small jaw and short canine teeth make the killing bite, crushing the victim's throat, difficult. The cheetahs, like the wild dog, hunt in the baking heat of the day to avoid what every animal fears most, the lion, and packs of roaming hyenas who are not bound to territory as even the lions are. The cheetah is not outmaneuvered by the impala, which it snares in a thicket. If the hunt is not successful, the cheetah would have to rest after its body overheats from the frantic short chase. The mother examines the lifeless impala then cries a short pattern of barks for the cubs who come running along. Five of them. Two or three or more will be dead soon, as most large litters do not survive their first year.

A large scarab beetle advances down the branch toward me. A small morsel indeed. But as the most adaptable of the big cats, I will eat many animals from termites to antelope. Whatever it takes to stay alive. That is why I can be found from the sultry rain forest, where I am master, to the steaming savannahs, where I must share my spoils. But to be the most adaptable, I have had to give up much. I have not the strength of the lion or speed of the cheetah, nor the communality of the hyenas. I hunt alone. A third the size of the lion, my strength is cunning agility.

A warthog piglet. I rise and loosen my body. The taint of pain from my right hindquarter reminds me why I am hungry, thirsty and in the notch of the tree without a kill to awaken to. I turn to inspect the damage. The wound is not completely healed, for that will take more time. But I am well enough not to be a banquet for flies and not stifled by pain to be concerned about my stride. I scan the plains. The herd is just stirring. The mother cheetah has found a spot to hide the carcass and watches her cubs eat.

The warthog piglet skirts the watering hole between giraffes and elephants. A white rhino shuffles about restlessly, distrusting and alert. There is no reason to the huge snorting animal's behavior, which seem at odds with order. Unlike the rest of those who live in the herd and are always searching over our shoulder, the rhino, like the elephant, has no natural enemies and no use for energies that might be expended to save its life.

I climb down, relieved that the pain and weakness has lessened. I am more of who I was, and less fearful of what I might have become. I will continue to favor the wound until it is completely healed. I am not even distracted or bothered by the flies and notice a collection of termite mounds lying between my tree and the watering hole. I make my way toward them, building confidence with each new stride. I leap to the crest of a mound whose height is almost the length of my body. The top is flattened, perfect for resting and surveying. Unlike lions and cheetahs that possess great skills of pursuit, leopards prefer to ambush prey. This requires a combination of patience and instincts found in few other plains animals.

I survey the kills that were made in the night, the time I once shared with the wild dogs. Roiling plumes of vultures dot the plains fighting over the remains of ibex, impala, wildebeests, topi, and other less fortunate. I am not as hungry as I thought I would be. The rest, not having to charge and replenish, stalk and ambush, the cool water and deep sleep have saved my life.

The piglet races about, frantic with fear. It knows not to bleat and alert nearby predators. Without protection from its mother, it will be picked off. A twinge of hunger. Perhaps I was wrong. But the distance is too great. Unless the creature comes directly to me, I will let it go, or watch a lion take it down. Then I hear it. The mother warthog, a formidable fighter with two razor tusks that outweighs most leopards. Still, she is moving in the wrong direction. Along the border of the herd and away from the watering hole and her child. But the piglet hears her and lifts his head and takes up a trot in her direction. He is moving directly towards me. There is nowhere to crouch or hide. If he sees me slip from the mound, it will distract him and he will run back towards the watering hole that is slowly filling up with the thirsty and vulnerable. Right towards me. An easy ambush, a quick killing bite, a certain meal.

The mother continues her misdirected search as the piglet approaches. By the time he sees me rise, it is too late. He gets off a sharp squeal and I am upon him. He thrashes about, but I am more than I was yesterday and he is no match for my powerful, experienced jaws. The killing bite crushes his throat. He squirms. Gasping for air, his heart pounds to make up the deficiency. Soon, the throbbing lessens until there is nothing. I get up and drag him to the tree, and then bound up into the notch where I spent the previous night.

He is larger than I first thought. I am relieved to see my wound does not limit my aggressiveness. I am exhausted, not by the kill, but by the anticipation of failure. I survey the plains for signs of unrest or curiosity that may have been stirred from my kill. Secure, I begin to eat. A lioness kills an ibex near the watering hole. If she had missed the ibex, she would surely have found the scent of the piglet. The mother warthog's call dissipates until I am left alone, carving out the animal's innards.

A pair of gray kestrels swoops down in pursuit of a vole caught too far from its earthen den. I have been that female kestrel. I have taken that vole back to my family. I have watched my children eat what I have set out before them. I do not recall the end of my life as a kestrel. Nor as any other animal. I just know I have been many.

I should have not been so distracted. It is already too late for me to react as the male lion approaches. He is the leader of the pride. His carriage and bearing tell me so, as it would any other. He looks up at me, not under the tree, but from a comfortable vantage point. A lioness joins him. They wait for my response. This confrontation has happened before. Once while my mother trained me and another time when I had taken a guinea fowl into a tree like this one. I pause defiantly, then rise and move down from branch to limb until only the drop to the grass remains. I look back at my half-eaten kill.

This is an act of pure arrogance since lions do not climb trees. They simply do not want me trespassing in their territory. And, if I do encroach, not be such an affront as to feed while they are near. The ibex kill brought them to the watering hole and bad luck brought them to me. Had they tracked the scent of the piglet that lead them to me? It does not matter. I hit the grass and walk submissively into the bush without the slightest intimation of injury, knowing they will not pursue. After a while, I turn, giving final notice of impudence and see something that I, nor other leopards I believe, have ever witnessed. The lioness parades around the tree with the arrogance of its breed then, in one vaulting leap, launches herself into the branches and snares the remains of the piglet. A shattered shadow in her massive jaws.

The male waits for the female to descend. She hesitates. Two other lionesses approach. Finally, she drops to the grass and the male and two other females tear at the tiny morsel dangling from the side of her mouth. In one powerful motion, she twists around and rips it away. A small piece of flesh protrudes from the jaws of the male. The remaining two females act out their frustration in mock combat for their loss of the kill. So powerful is the drive to feed that failure is not dictated by amount, but by prestige.

But I am satisfied and know that I only have to make one more kill soon, to live through my wound. I must have been moving along at a quick pace for I find myself ahead of the grazing herd. It does not concern me. I have passed the scent markings of lions, cheetahs, and hyenas as well as a leopard. It may be a brother or sister my mother has spawned.

There is a calm about me that was not present yesterday, as it was before the encounter with the lion. I will hunt differently now, though I do not know how long that caution will last. I have become more respectful of circumstances the most skilled hunters cannot control. I am aware of this and more; certainly that I was fortunate to survive a wound I have seen hobble greater beasts. These same circumstances favored my recovery, and I have been granted the value of experiences from other lives beyond a mere scattering of unconnected recollections.

As the land warms and gray clouds wither, territorial boundaries become vague and float to the needs of the predators. Many prides and packs will rather die than leave their territory knowing that it will not be unoccupied when they return. The rains finally abandon the grasslands. Before the seasons change again, many will perish in the wake of the heat and unbearable thirst. Fires will sear the plains, killing grass and in the process, replenishing. Cubs will litter the savannah, a reminder of what parents will sacrifice so that they may live to create another, stronger, more fortunate generation.

Swarms of vultures will outnumber the flies, whose tormenting mass explodes on the bounty of death. I have seen ibex wilt from the heat, elephants driven mad with thirst and exhaustion, and lions with gaping, slashing wounds that could have only been made from one of their own, stagger from the shade of one juniper to the other until they're bled dry. Death has many ways of taking less willful souls such as black crowned cranes, secretary birds, and bustards that follow the great herds in anticipation of the insect life that is kicked up by their hooves.

Soon fur begins to grow beneath the wound and replenish my yellow markings. Like most, I will grow weary of the baking sun. But I will survive the dry times watching from an acacia, a juniper, and a hillock. Waiting with my memories of fox, impala, fowl, hogs, oryx, and snakes. Taking whatever I find into the trees and never forgetting the lioness whose instinct carried her beyond the boundaries of her species. I feel a little more vulnerable, slightly less in command of myself. I have passed through the worst of it.

With the end of the season, as I wait for the rains to wash away the scent markings, fill the lagoons and seal the mudflats, rejuvenate the monkeys and giant forest hog, instill hope into vast numbers of cormorants, geese, plovers, sandpipers, gulls, and terns, I am left to think of what I may have been, and what I may become in my next life—a bird, a bat, a cape buffalo, a predator lurking in the waterways, or raptor in the skies, or possibly a black rhino or wistfully, a lion, and I am left with the fear that I may return as the creature I dread most, the beast that kills for the teeth of the elephant.

The Cracked Goblet

Come with me. Yes. Right down there. The path can be quite treacherous, and we have so little daylight left. The road forks, just there. I know it well. I will not forsake you.

You look wary. I should have given you my unquestioned candor. It is my fault. Your steadfast resolve in my behalf has always given me worthy comfort. I have enjoyed your favor and have given you in return—what—shall we say—greater cause for concern?

I hear that your continued praise in spite of my behavior, which, I can only agree with the critics, or scoundrels, that it does no one good to associate with me. Yet you persist resolutely in my defense. And how it has suffered recently, as have many a vulgar dramatist at the sharpened blade of my opinion.

My wrath used to be more accentuated, more potent. "Vigorous with venomous condemnation" I overheard at a party. Not at all balanced by compassion and guidance, as it should be if I possessed greater sensitivity to the gravity with which my ruling was regarded.

Instead, I inspire terror in many who wished to pick up a pen knowing that my gaze might fall on their scratch. Knowing that I may come to their prose with too much drink the previous night or worse, abstinence from grog, anger not offset from the work that spread before me on previous days or, more treacherously, envy. And the younger and more personable they were, or had they already received piddling notoriety, I was compelled to attack with a vengeance that startled.

Sure of the torture and obstacles and his own frailties, Balzac, a well-received contemporary, though I am sure you are not familiar with his work, it is rumored, chained himself to his chair and retired from mingling in order to compose *La Comédie humaine.*

Yes, a moral traditionalist and a reactionary in politics, the sardonic Frenchman offers the human character as circumscribed, but finely influenced by its hereditary, geographical, historical, and social environment. *La Comédie humaine*, a most prodigious volume of 2,000 recurring characters encompassing five decades of post-revolutionary France elucidating principles that govern society and those which are concerned with the motives behind human behavior.

A remarkable treatise, an absorbing commentary on the human tragedy, a biting exposition that is regrettably wasted on even those few who have read it. Too many think they can achieve equally without unreserved sacrifice.

Pray, pause. You do not want to go there, my loyal friend. An ambush of forest, thickets, and grasping vines, an ideal rampart for strangers poised to misdirect you along this treacherous terrain.

And you must believe what I say, not like some men that have passed our way recently. We are true to contract and vows and cannot be broken by speculation, wager, or doubt.

Not that I refuse to indulge my own peculiarities whenever opportunity sparkles, as do we both. A stout drink, a sumptuous breast, leg, or hip, pink painted lips and variety in abundant flesh.

We are men of the world, putting niggardly difference aside so that the greater cause can be mediated in our own behalf. That is, after all, why we have come together this inhospitable, outcast day, to have success at what opportunities have been placed in our path.

Not as treacherous one as the one underfoot, not as wet and slippery and winding and dark with hidden consequence as the turn you nearly chose just now, but a rich and adulterous prize that is well within our means. With our intent renewed and challenged, we shall have it and partake of the riches waiting before us. We are the only two who could benefit from such a morsel and the only two whose combined talent, shall I—shall we—say would, when combined, make the most of the treasures afoot.

Here, let's not quibble over whom is the quickest or wisest to first finger the game—lame and vulnerable or hearty though given to moral inadequacies. Is it not enough that we are both possessed of acumen and rigor to set aside difference, immodest naturally, so that our pleasures and craft may be truly rewarded?

The veins in your neck dilated with apprehension as soon as we departed my carriage in the bramble off the main road and started on foot. They are now restful, uncoiled. I have noticed that in some men, the jugular, I have learned they call it, standing on the sides of your throat and when pressed upon by collar or agitated by deed, becomes engorged and throbs with distrust.

Now stop, take back a breath, as heartily as if it was your last, and gaze about you. Not twenty leagues from London and we are secluded in forests that were here for ages beyond count. The sky, billowing white when we set out, is now steely gray. It urges us to make haste.

And you are a noticeably tamer, more patient, and tolerant than I am. You believe in the human spirit and "civility" and "tenacity"—your two favorite words—while my summation of human nature begins and ends at "mendacity." And, coming from a fairly well-to-do family, you were not deprived of an education and have none of the scars I have accumulated from elevating myself beyond established ranks.

While you scuttered about wagging your tongue at professors who could not care if you had drowned in your inkwell, I mastered thought and word and mistrusted deed which, by the way, I believe has been the more honest tutor.

I admire your bravery this day, and on such short notice. For that, you have my gratitude, though I am not to be trusted when it comes to controlling my passion for the sufferance of others. You again have me there. I shall take your abuse knowing that it is payment and long overdue for the other travails to which my instability has subjected you.

I will not do penance which is so popular today, casting aside inequalities and flaws simply by avowing them in public. You know from what I speak and to whom I am taking note here.

We both have seen his tendencies to provoke and abuse. He has degraded and given false promise and testimony. And for that, he shall receive a fate due his sins. I believe in the equity of the hereafter to reach out and take him.

You are skeptical of my appetite for revenge, though you have uttered such indignities in your mind before entering bed and stealing a cold hand to your wife's plentiful buttocks.

No, please, there will be time. You will know the nature of our scheme when we can look each other over a glass of port in the foreground of a stern fire.

For these last three fortnights, we have labored under the eyes of family and authorities and have not come to suspicion, advancing further than was prudent and this among all else is the hallmark of our greatness. Immodesty.

On the list of failings of those who have come before us and those who will take up our cudgel, this may be the most difficult path to cultivate. Immodesty leads one to boldness and boldness not reigned in leads to imprudence and miscalculation.

Yes. Grand impudence and arrogance marks the headstone of the fool. A short-lived genus that tramples opportunity and mocks the misfortune of others.

Right there. Up ahead. Yes. The stone house with untended gardens and fountains abutting the ample servants stall. It is empty now, abandoned and, until recently, taken over by one Arthur Wexton, a rather rotund, self-engaging, squalid little sugar merchant.

Twenty-one years he labored with family and malaria and dysentery and cholera and he prevailed, as we have, through hard work and fortune, made himself a man of imposing substance. He is not there now and will not be set to assume the manor house until work is completed.

The umbrella of boughs unfolds above. Quite

an alliteration, I must say. Quite a poet I have become in my brief tenure of sobriety. And who is to say to the contrary? I will have no man as my critic, as I was born to be his.

I must rest here. We are no longer as young as we might be to make this trip on one gulp of wind. We have both prospered and strike us one fault if it is not to wine or flesh; it is to sustenance that we are both forgiven. Fortunately, overeating is a chink that will not land us in debtor's prison, though if we were to continue at this rate we might not be able to fit through the oaken doors of Newgate Prison itself regardless of the venality of our offense.

Money lavished on this fine residence will bring it to a golden halo of respectability. Money, I am told, that drained from the harnessed necks of beaten slaves that nourished the soil that produced the crops that went to a begging market that were sold at such a prodigious profit that this Wexton fellow acquired more land by muzzle, brutality, and fabrication until its perimeter could only be measured by the boundaries of heaven.

He is a man of wealth. Nothing more. While we possess character and connivance, experience and trust.

You are dumbstruck. Excitement rings in your heart. A strike of some substance, I would say, and when the adroitness of my inspiration is understood, you will be even more surprised.

Moreover, if you were not so diligent at keeping yourself from losing control underfoot, though you hardly had a choice, you might have noticed the sentry on duty to the left of the main entrance watching us as we crossed the clearing overgrown with weed and time.

I am in jest, though not at all. Only a raven my friend. Planted there on a split bough. As fat and as black as the night or the heart of the master of this estate. Black as coal—or his future.

Perched and awaiting, and if you are superstitious, and who among us is not, a sign of good fortune. We are but passing through, therefore he is not a sentry for us, only a well-placed lookout. He will warn us if there is reason. We will hear his scream. His warning. I am keyed to his pitch already.

Sir, your shoulder. The weather has changed the temper of the wood and requires our combined effort. Your shoulder again. Once more and, there, we are in. It is done. Your hesitation as we came out of the underbrush and were confronted with the formidability of Lord Wexton's acquisition should diminish for we have nothing to fear.

An impressive abode. You are adequately affected. Excellent. However, strange shapes frozen in form or the echoes of inequities that cloud this chamber must not divert our attention.

Forgive the trust that swims so freely between us, but there was motive for my actions to which you will soon be privy. For now, I shall—yes, here they are, two small torches, and thusly we will make our way to a room I have chosen for our task.

Rats afoot. Take note. The good Lord Wexton, as he has purchased—at considerable sum I am told—a title befitting his temperament and wealth, will make them his allies soon enough.

This way now. No mud or tendrils or branches, just worn stone stairs leading down into a room I have not yet branded with reason. Here. Am I not a man of my word? Have you ever been in such a secluded, temporarily pleasant sanctuary as this? Cling to your torch and we will partake of a surprise, to you that is, and then down to business.

Your delight is evident even in shadows of doubt. And in the shade of shadows, we shall plot and you shall sit and be relieved of the strain across your belly. No, you are quite right, and I am unpardonable in my excessive reference, but I am dependent on you and your long life in our behalf and for that, you must excuse my overbearing attentiveness to the threat of your girth.

A last twisting passageway and we will be there. Slowly, ever so carefully, for the corridor narrows down those stairs as though deciding who will and will not pass. It has a religious tone, selecting, embracing one over the other. Who shall be admitted and who shall remain an outsider? Who shall live and who shall die? Perhaps my exaggerated reference to your waistline was a harbinger. Had you been too large to maneuver through this passageway, then you might never set to the plot.

I can only wonder if there is such a thing as good over evil in the world in which we are tasked. Evil has marked the land as if no other ethereal force existed. I am not a religious man by nature and the reference to the almighty is made more out of fear than respect.

At last, our journey's reward. Not the room, for it is spare and chill, sunk in the bowels of the land under the manor. But another indulgence I have prepared for this occasion. You are positively dissolved in sweat and exhaustion. Sit there and set the torch at your side and I will see to preparations.

Do you think me too theatrical or that I eagerly succumb to the superciliousness of my craft or refuse to examine my own shallow pretentious masquerade?

And what of your craft? Is it more or less better or worse, humbler or grander than another? Is it no better to slaughter cows, sheep, and pigs, strip them of their identity, yank out their hearts, cut into their soul, and leave them hanging so that flies may be offered hearty refuge?

What other choice did you have, to elevate yourself even though you had not turned to it agreeably, but conveniently reaped the whirlwind of your grandfather's energy and sacrifice? You'll agree of course, these things are so, well, subjective.

Here, with my torch you can see the difference. A curious rat or unnatural force has conspired against us for there is only one goblet that has not been tainted. I took two from the crate when I came upon this house and set them with this fine port as a reward for our journey. Yet my generosity for our pleasure has not been totally undermined. Not at all. For we shall say, for the moment, at least for then, that you are my guest in this grand style and you shall have the best of whatever I possess.

You are the best of our partnership, a family man, trusted and admired in the community and as a cohort you have given to me as no other, and you shall have the sounder goblet. I cleared this oaken table during my last visit and it has remained so. We will have at its center our plot and our port and our pleasure.

A toast then. To what? Pause and reflect because this salute under this stonework and rampart will be prelude to what I have in store for our future. Therefore it must be a pledge that deserves thought and is without contrivance or triviality.

Since I have arranged this banquet and given rise to our party, it is my duty to—no, my friend, I will not injure myself on the irregular portion. I will drink from the other side; you will drink from your own fine glass, and with the other eye watch and make certain the shattered half in my hand does not interfere with the toast at my lips.

To our future. To our continued good fortune and let no act of man or God set us apart.

And, I survive uncut and warmed at once. Fine wine is at the center of candor and deportment. Excellent. And well spoken. Who said that? Some fine philosopher I would say, or one part of a pair about to commence a deed that shall change his—our lives forever. I fear that one bottle, fine as it may be, may not be adequate for the length of our stay.

Sir, another full glass for your thirst, which must surely have suffered with the complex meanderings of our journey. I should tell you that this route, though circuitous and unnatural, leaving my carriage abandoned by the roadside as you pointed out more than once, had reason behind purpose. Cunning if you will. I delight in affecting such conundrums, as you are aware.

You, I am sure would have taken the more direct route and certainly we would have arrived refreshed and long before dusk. And I would have applauded your choice, but now I ask your dispensation. For the nature of our journey suits my overly secretive and circumspect nature.

Oh, wonderful, then you shall have a go at it my friend and we shall toast, another time and in approbation to the raven. To the raven, may he watch over us with orderly reverence.

But, to continue, I have learned that this man Wexton is not simply a sugar baron who squanders his wealth on tapestries and lordly trappings. He is a man of considerable influence that can be traced and translated into the very corridors of political power to the commerce which we both are beholden. And to which we have on many occasions debased our character and given pretense as long as it benefited our enterprise.

It seems that Lord Wexton, one wife, four children, a sickly father, and a surfeit of servants and mistress in tow, was cultivating excesses long before arriving on these shores. And in the task of cultivating the earth and ears of the powerful, he was equally gifted.

A skilled manipulator of fate and fortune from thousands of miles in languid tropics we can only envy. So when he arrived, his importance was already a factor to consider. There! The glint is widening. I knew it. You are too smart and wise in the ways of political propensities for this man to have eluded your attention. Maybe it was the manor or port, or my good, if equally dissipated nature that brought the connection to these circumstances clearly before you. A combination then or other beyond my knowledge.

But, have I offended you. Surely, the vintage remains in your favor. We have that much left and more. And, as always, you are welcome to my share.

Sir, you are unsettled. Your eyes narrow and betray your discomfort. Your hands are equally agitated. Has the nature of this tomb and the convoluted journey that brought us to this location undermined your equilibrium, causing you to suspect I have overstepped my bounds?

I thought you might know this Wexton fellow, but it was of coincidence, not conflict. Do you wish me to continue or do you have something you would prefer to add that might clarify or sway my unflattering opinion of the man?

That you knew him was never in doubt here. Moreover, that should be none of my concern. You have other interests and dealings as have I. In addition, it is to our wiser nature to be employed in as many profitable ventures as we can master. Only good sense there too. I drink from a cracked goblet and all to machinations that have brought us such prosperity.

But, you do not join me!

Positively, I have somehow offended you? Have I insulted you simply by associating your name with that of this pernicious rascal? This purveyor of mistrust and unsound intentions. That I bear him no personal ill will is obvious, but only because his tendencies have not subordinated my interests. If I found that he was in such a position and used his influence to undermine mine then, of course, I would want him no good fortune. And, as with everything, of course we would share that sentiment.

Is that not true?

And if he corrupted what you had prepared, would I not want him exposed? Would I not stand at your side at such a time?

Again, you refuse to respond to what must be a mundane inquiry. I see from your reserve that you have affixed yourself to a position and cannot, or will not, be diverted.

You know, good port demands, or at least I have heard, it is more palatable if taken in fine glasses. A perfect pair of gilded, crystal Venetian or Austrian goblets would more suit the occasion. A send off, as such. These in our possession are weak, brittle and inarticulate and notably insufficient to the substance of this grape. An added burden for your refined tastes at an awkward moment like this, I am sure.

But my efforts to divert your disquietude have failed. I am not good at subtle diversion. Never have been. For I am too forthright, too open and unveiled in countenance. Not like so many that one tends to consider a friend. Lord Wexton has many friends, or so I have heard. Many who count him in league in high places, as well devotees in common places. I wonder in which you feel most comfortable.

Now there, you might want to pause and reflect before responding. All eyes fixed on the truth here. I will drink to the truth. Sir, to candor, character, and conduct befitting friendship. Good friends. Old friends. Confidantes who work together in each other's best interest, or not at all

But I seemed to have provoked you further. I shall pour myself a final glass and you will finish off the bottle. No? There is still adequate supply to fill your goblet, the one with the smooth, uncorrupted rim.

No. I suppose not. Then I will drink alone. Well, not quite alone. Rats abound underfoot. They do prowl about, you know, when they sense quietude or weakness, an enemy handcuffed, a meal, hamstrung overhead for the taking.

Is the conversation, or monologue as it has turned out to be, not to your liking? It offends your ear, your cultured taste? I can readily understand that. But better to be out with it and bring whatever moistened agitation to your forehead then let the plan remain secret—yours and Lord Wexton's, I mean—forever.

Then it seems your allegiance at my expense, of course, far outweighs your word. A contradiction don't you think? Our natural instincts, interchangeable and yet quite distinct have worked so well and have brought us quite more than we ever deserved.

Now deceit, or would you prefer a less confrontational representation of your treachery?

Be still. Again, be quite still. No good deed ever goes undone. Or is it, no bad deed goes unpunished?

My memory was never a suit I played well. Although memory is not a question here. Deceit, naked and fundamental, is what has brought us to Lord Wexton's future residence. And deceit is—well, what can be said of it except that it bears a striking resemblance to conceit. Conceit, you have frequently admitted, often with a pride that escapes me, is a cloak you wear tightly to your chest.

A brother, as you have become to this fine fellow who spreads his sticky, sugary wealth to ensnare the soul of others. And, has he succeeded? Well, of course there is room for speculation in high places, but not here. Not in this place. Not in this room. Not over this table where you have learned not only of my knowledge but how, as a prancing connoisseur, to drink fine port.

Be still. Not a word. I insist!

Indignation is a tiresome ploy. And the mask of outrage is wasted here, as is self-righteous indignation, another of your gross indulgences.

Your pupils are dilated, exposing what, good sir? Evil? Malignant and pernicious evil? What else could I claim? What else could you deny? What a stage you make of your outrage, of your contempt that others cower so easily. I have seen it, and once, I too was impressed.

What else have you been hiding? What else indeed. Acquisitiveness? Avarice? The cancer of unrestrained moral turpitude? What else can we say of my friend with whom trust is a bond "never to be breached?" Your pledge, sealed with your handshake as we departed our last meeting. Your words, not those of an "overzealous, uninspired pedantic" as I have recently been informed you refer to me in mixed company.

You look surprised. Positively shocked. Did you think the jagged rim of my goblet would be as dull as you and your half-witted, canting friend have taken me for, or the possiblility that I would not waste a rare vintage simply to slit your throat?

How have you misjudged me so badly? None is so misunderstood than those we take for granted, you fat seething scoundrel.

There, then. Finality. It is done.

Your grasping hands will not staunch the spurting red flow, for I have struck as practiced, as you offered me the most extravagant target of a guilt fattened vein, the grandmaster of blue coiling, throbbing guilt. It is but a nick, say, not an inch long. Though, length here is not the issue, nearly as important as depth.

My cut to you is as deep as you've ever been my friend, and as deep as you will ever be. So in death, I have branded you with character. What humor is stillborn in that wit?

I am not impressed with your selection of words, poorly considered as phrases are unconvincing, even your expression lacks theatrical style. Unfortunately, there is no one here to hear your garbled, panicked, pleas.

Hear their squeal? Your essence has wetted their palate. Stained their fur and teased their appetite, so to speak. Not a very good pun, but then I am badly distressed that I lost so much fine wine in the transaction.

I should think even now you would grow slightly dizzy. Tingling in your fingertips may present a minor distraction. Your bladder will not hold its own much longer. And already your feet grow cold, deadened to the eager movement about them. Your heart pounds hysterically, but in a theater spared an approving audience.

And for what? A few more pounds of sterling from Wexton? Another twisting scheme to compound the last, to show yourself capable of cleverness, ingenious trickery, betraying others, denying decency, loyalty and promulgating, of all things, "civility?"

Sit where you are!

Your efforts to dislodge yourself from this regrettable plight will come to no avail, as will the fruits of your chicanery with your conspirator. Or that you will live another hour to wedge yourself in between the legs of some unsuspecting woman, torment your sons, flog your servants, cheat a creditor, or betray a friend.

I suppose such a frenzied, frothing sight would be repugnant to most. As for me, I would only have preferred if it had happened sooner, though even now I am sure that the lord of this cursed manor will not notice your loss as much as you might want.

However, it may be important to Lord Wexton's future in this county, more than an inconvenience when the authorities find your body, or the chewed remains of it in his wine cellar. How coincidental. A well-placed word, even by an overzealous pedantic, may start an inquiry which may lead to an investigation which, if directed with adroitness, will most assuredly lead to fatal embarrassment. And then who will pay for the excess above us and family while he languishes in prison?

What must you think of me now? What indeed? "What *has* he done to me?" you ask with tortured, tremulous tongue. "How could he do this to me?" you say. A friend.

Don't you toy with that word, not even in jest. Not ever again—a friend—not ever again.

I will spare you further chagrin and be off. As you know, my carriage is a brisk walk from here in daylight and in weather so uncertain, it may be formidable. So I must capture the waning dusk. I wouldn't want to lose a heel, twist an ankle, stumble, and fall knowing that you will not be there to catch me.

Of course, you understand the rest of the wine is yours. Enjoy. Let it cool and refresh.

No sir. Pray, please don't get up. I am well acquainted with the route of my return.

I'll take the torches and, oh yes, of course, my empty goblet. For it is broken, dangerous in fact, and regrettably has no practical use. In passing, as you might as well retain some satisfaction from this stressful encounter and know, though I am sure it will soon be forgotten, that I am fearful of the dark and this experience has called up all my courage to complete.

Undoubtedly, I should not have divulged that secret. You know how keen I am about privacy. Though I suspect that this, among all else, is eternally in your good safekeeping, as is the key in my hand that will secure the hardened oak door as I leave, in my good safekeeping.

Good night then, good friend. Good night.

Arthur Davis is a management consultant specializing in corporate planning and reorganization and has been quoted in The New York Times, Crain's New York Business and interviewed on New York TV News Channel 1. He has taught at The New School University, advised The New York City Taxi & Limousine Commission on organizational reform, advised Senator John McCain's investigating committee on boxing reform, appeared as an expert witness on best practices in 1999 before State Senator Roy Goodman's New York State Commission on Corruption in Boxing, advised the Department of Homeland Security, National Protection and Programs Directorate and lectures on leadership skills to CEO's and entrepreneurs.

He has written over 130 tales of horror, dark fantasy, slipstream, science fiction, speculative fiction, crime, epic adventure, magical realism as well as literary/mainstream fiction. Since 2012, sixty have been published in forty online and print journals including The Missing Slate (Story of The Month), Allegory, The Colored Lens, Crack the Spine (Anthology), Eunoia, Menacing Hedge, Front Porch Review, The Amsterdam Review (Reading) and Black Fox Literary Magazine. A dozen more have been published as reprints, and "Conversation in Black" was nominated for the 2015 Pushcart Prize.

www.ingramcontent.com/pod-product-compliance
Lightning Source LLC
Chambersburg PA
CBHW060634130626
46555CB00002B/790